Of Things G

Janina Matthewson.

Of Things Gone Astray.

The Friday Project
An imprint of HarperCollins*Publishers*
1 London Bridge Street
London SE1 9GF

www.harpercollins.co.uk

First published by The Friday Project in 2014
This paperback edition first published 2015

A catalogue record for this book is available from the British Library

ISBN: 978-0-00-810037-7

For Ronnie

Mrs Featherby.

MRS FEATHERBY HAD BEEN HAVING pleasant dreams until she woke to discover the front of her house had vanished overnight.

They had been dreams of when she was younger and more energetic, dreams of a time when she had full use of her knees. She had saved someone in one of them, someone helpless, she thought, but once awake she couldn't remember who or why or what had happened next.

It was the breeze that woke her, naturally. It wasn't that it was a cold breeze, or even a particularly strong one, but when a person has gone to sleep in perfect stillness, the unexplained movement of air around the room is a rousing influence, and Mrs Featherby had never been a deep sleeper.

She looked around her for a moment in that state of bewilderment that often occurs in the moments after waking. The light from the street was flooding into the room through the gaping hole that the previous evening had been her bedroom wall. Mrs Featherby blinked hard twice and decided to pull herself together. She stepped out of her bed and walked to the edge of the floor, the wind whipping the hem of her ancient nightgown and pulling at her long, flint-coloured hair.

It was early, barely five o'clock, so there were no people around, but Mrs Featherby knew that when there were people, those people would stare. She knew that they might even approach the house. That they might ask questions. That they might attempt to breach the sanctity of her home, of her fortress. She set her mouth and turned away.

Mrs Featherby, whose first name was Wendy, or had been many years earlier, did not waste time in wondering how a tonne of brick and mortar could have been uplifted and transported away without waking her or leaving a trace of masonry on the road. She did what was practical and called the police. She didn't particularly trust the police, but she felt that it was the correct procedure.

She was informed that an officer would be sent within the hour, so, thanking her stars that the bathroom was at the back of the house, she performed her ablutions efficiently and impeccably and moved downstairs to the sitting room to wait.

She wondered if she should have anything ready for the constable when he arrived. She'd always considered herself lucky to not have had the police in her home before, but the downside to this was becoming apparent: she had no idea of the correct etiquette.

Indeed, it had been so long since she'd had anyone of any kind in the house that she'd all but forgotten how to go about it. The only person that had crossed her threshold in recent months was the young man who delivered her groceries at nine fifteen every Tuesday.

Was it correct, Mrs Featherby wondered, to refer to the impending officer of the law as a guest? If he was to be a guest she should certainly have, at the very least, a cup of tea waiting, and possibly a biscuit. The cake she'd made on Sunday had been past its best yesterday and she'd thrown it out. She had intended to bake a replacement, but doing so before seven in the morning simply for the imminent arrival of an officer of the law seemed a little extravagant. And he might arrive in the middle of the process, which would be entirely inappropriate. She would make some biscuits later in the day, she decided, as she'd intended. There was no need to rush the process.

Tea would do, she decided. Tea would be enough.

Mrs Featherby sat still and upright in her chair, gazing through her absence of wall into the garden beyond. She sat still and upright and waited.

Cassie.

CASSIE WAS LIT FROM WITHIN, or so she felt. She gloried for a moment in how little she cared about the strangers that surrounded her, that may have noticed her. Let them look, she thought, let them marvel at her secret joy. Let them recognise her as one of the few for whom life holds wonder. For it must be only a few, she thought, who are designed to know this kind of exultation. If it were everyone, the earth's orbit would be altered by it, forever thrown off course by the collective gladness of its inhabitants.

Her eyes seemed to throb with the smile hidden behind them. The corners of her mouth were set in a curve that any moment threatened to beam.

Cassie ran a hand through her hair and looked at the arrivals board.

IB2202 from São Paulo: LANDED

The letters rearranged themselves: FLOSS IS HERE.

Cassie had been playing this moment over in her mind for weeks. Months. All her life. There were many versions.

There was the one where Floss ran through the gate, paused for a moment on her toes, scanning the crowd like a blithe and confident huntress, until she spotted Cassie and soared into her arms.

There was the version where she walked through slowly and carefully, not even looking at Cassie till they were six inches apart, but smiling all the while.

4

There was the version where she stopped as soon as she'd come through and the two of them stand there for fully five minutes, for forever, just looking. Staring at each other, right in the eyes, across the space between them, both knowing they have an eternity in which to touch.

Now, though, now it was moments away, she couldn't imagine anything at all. All she could do was wait and watch.

IB2202 from São Paulo: LANDED

Cassie watched the steady stream of people walking through the gate. She wondered how many planes had recently landed and how many passengers there were on each plane and what the statistical likelihood was of Floss being the next person through at any given point. She knew it was stupid, but it thrilled her to think that the odds were rising with each reunion.

IB2202 from São Paulo: LANDED

There was a child crying. Cassie watched. The girl's mother was trying to make her hug her father, but she wouldn't. He was in uniform and Cassie wondered if he'd been away so long his daughter had forgotten him.

The crowd around her thinned and swelled again.

Cassie hadn't noticed, but the corners of her mouth were no longer curved. She gazed at the gate.

A flight attendant led through a boy of about seven. His mother hugged him briefly, cautiously, and took his bag.

IB2202 from São Paulo had disappeared from the arrivals board to make way for other flights.

A woman jostled Cassie in an attempt to get to a tanned teenage girl with a pack on her back. Cassie planted her feet more firmly on the floor.

She planted her feet and waited.

She gazed at the gate.

Delia.

DELIA TRIED TO BE QUIET, she tried really hard, but there was that door, that one door, the one into the kitchen, which always, every time, in spite of her best efforts, banged just a little as she closed it.

'Bloody bollocks,' she muttered, screwing her eyes closed and waiting.

It was thirty seconds before the tremulous 'Dee?' floated down the hall, but it felt longer. Still, it was always going to come, obviously.

'Morning, Mum,' Delia called back. 'Go back to sleep. I'm heading out for a couple of hours. Not long. I'll be back to make breakfast before you're ready to get up.'

'Why? Why are you going out? It's so early.'

Delia fought the urge to answer with a petulant 'I do what I want'.

'It's a clear morning, Mum,' she said instead. 'There's not another forecast for ages.'

Delia waited hopefully, barely breathing, until she was sure there was going to be no further reply. She grabbed her bag off the floor, where she'd left it in preparation, and let herself out. The heavy front door was so much easier to control than the flighty ones inside.

The two girls who lived together over the road, the ones Delia always thought seemed about twelve, were coming back from a party, turning into their house casually, as if this was a perfectly normal thing to be doing shortly after five o'clock in the morning on a weekday. Watching them, Delia felt immediately that she was always, and by nature, simultaneously underdressed and wearing too many clothes. She didn't remember ever going out with so little covered, not even in what she had always considered a comparatively wild first year of university.

She wondered briefly what was going on with teenagers these days, whether they ever properly considered the impression they were making on the world, before she felt suddenly that she was in danger of turning into the worst kind of maiden aunt. At least, she would be if she had any brothers or sisters. The worst kind of nosy spinster. If she continued on this way, she'd end up a bitter old woman who lived alone and never spoke to anyone. Who resented the laughter she heard on the street because it interrupted her peaceful, isolated days; trapped in a prison of her own bitterness, she'd wither and die and no one would know.

She sighed, and resolved, not for the first time, to be less judgemental of how stupid all the young people were. To be less judgemental in general. After all, those girls couldn't have been twelve – they lived alone, that would be ridiculous. Probably they were twenty, maybe even as old as twenty-two. They may have been at high school at the same time as Delia. If they'd gone to the same school, she could have been their prefect. She could have told them that skirts are traditionally worn to conceal the buttocks, rather than to reveal them, and that they can actually do so and still look quite alluring. Presuming that still held true, of course; Delia suddenly felt unsure.

As she wended her way through the neighbourhood, Delia began constructing a detailed fantasy in which the two girls ran into a string of amusing mishaps, and came to Delia for advice. They looked at her in wide-eyed gratitude as she dispensed the theories she held on life and love and the world, that a serious lack of life experience had thus far prevented her from proving correct.

She walked with a kind of sick eagerness. It had rained brutally for the last two weeks, leaving her in dire need of escape.

7

There was a small square on a small hill a short walk away from the house. Delia planned to sit in it, on a certain bench, and breathe the air, and let the world wake around her.

After half an hour she realised to her surprise that, instead of being at the small square, she was drawing close to the much larger park. She was disconcerted, the park wasn't anywhere near the square, she couldn't figure out how she'd got there. Probably she'd just not been paying attention to where she was going. Her feet had heard park and her head had said square and the two hadn't communicated. She told herself to be more of a grown up, and headed into the park.

This was a park she'd once gone to every fine day.

There was a picnic rug she used to take, and a thermos, and a basket with room for books as well as food to last her hours. She'd sit near a particular tree, an oak tree, moving in and out of the shade every so often, books and notes spread out around her, which she'd weighed down with rocks to stop them flying away.

Being outside had made her feel like her studying was less fevered and panicked. It had made her feel like the stakes were lower, or as if the outcome was already assured. When she was outside, even if it was the day before an exam, it felt like a gentle, pleasant pastime, rather than a stressful and emotionally fraught step on the way to her happy and successful future. She always did better with assignments and tests when the weather was fine. When she'd moved away to university, she'd spent an entire month trying to find a tree as effective as the one in this park.

Delia wandered through the park looking around; suddenly she wanted to find her old study tree. Maybe she'd read beside it for a while. Maybe she'd just sit there and watch the sun rise. She walked around what she thought was the entire park without finding it, wondering if maybe it had been cut down. Of course that was a ridiculous thing to think; the tree had been large and healthy, and if someone had been foolish enough to slay it, there would have been a giant tree trunk in place of the tree itself.

Delia was becoming petulant. The tree, her tree, didn't seem to be anywhere. She felt betrayed, as if the park, unhappy at her long absence, had reconfigured itself like a labyrinth, had made itself a stranger to her. She walked round and round and up and down, until, frustrated, she threw herself down on the top of the hill in the middle of the park. She drew her knees up and buried her face in her crossed arms.

She stayed like that for several moments, before raising her head and looking out.

The clear dawn that had been promised turned out to be twenty minutes of low morning sun before a bank of clouds swallowed the light. The city was now spread grey before her, but Delia kind of liked it that way.

She knew her mother would be up soon, and she knew she should be there to help her, but she couldn't resist staying a while longer. She would only be ten minutes. Ten minutes couldn't hurt.

Robert.

IT WAS AS IF THE alarm clock had gone off. But it hadn't. Robert lay, blinking, feeling the ring echo in his ears as if he'd heard it moments before. But he hadn't.

Mara was asleep beside him, her face serious in a way it never was when she was awake. The light of the alarm clock spilled across her forehead.

5:07

Robert was at a loss. He hated being inactive and he very rarely was. There was always something to do. There was always an excess of things to do. But not at just after five in the morning.

He groaned with frustration, and then grimaced with guilt and glanced at Mara. She slept on.

Robert carefully slid out of bed. He'd go for a run. It had been months since he'd found the time, and here the time was, gifted to him out of nowhere. He hunted out his battered running shoes, the same he'd had since university, and changed into an old t-shirt and shorts.

The air was clear and easy to breathe, and Robert felt energised and enthusiastic as he jogged past the silent houses on his street.

After half a mile a frown crossed his face. This was harder than he'd thought it would be.

He jogged onward.

He reached a nearby park and slipped inside to run on the grass, feeling a moment of relief as his knees registered the absence of concrete. Then he promptly developed a stitch.

He came to a panting halt and bent over, clutching his sides. Taking a couple of breaths, he staggered on.

By the time he got back home, his face was red and streaming and he was limping. He stood outside the house for two minutes, arms akimbo, gasping for air, before he opened the door and dragged himself upstairs. As he walked into the bedroom Mara stirred and opened her eyes. She blinked at him a couple of times and burst out laughing.

Robert poked his tongue out at her and headed for the bathroom.

'You shouldn't laugh you know,' he said over his shoulder. 'This is me recognising the need to hang onto you by maintaining a slammin' bod.'

'Oh god, please don't take my laughter as a sign I'm not grateful.'

'I'll fill your grate,' Robert said. 'Be quiet and let me shower, woman.'

He could hear Mara chuckling into her pillow as he closed the bedroom door on her, trying to make sure she didn't see him wince.

Marcus.

BIRDS. DIDN'T FEEL LIKE TIME yet. Didn't feel late enough for birds. But there they were, so that was that. Birds could sense time better than him, so they must be right.

He opened his eyes. Ah. There was the problem. The blinds were down. He usually slept with them open, he usually woke with the light.

Strange. That they were closed.

He sat up and slid on his glasses. He crossed to the window and opened the blinds. It was later than he'd thought. It was later than he usually woke up. It was much later.

He had a routine for the mornings. Always the same. A light breakfast of fruit. A full breakfast later, after some time in the music room. Now it wouldn't work. Now it had gone wrong. It was already too late.

He went downstairs and stood in the kitchen. He was hungrier than usual. He opened the fridge and took out the eggs.

It wasn't until almost eight o'clock that he made it to the music room. Much later than normal.

The music room was the nicest room in the house. It was the most important place in the house. Floor to ceiling windows along two walls. Lots of light. He liked lots of light to practise, although when he performed he always requested that the stage be kept as dim as possible. People should be listening, he said, not looking.

When he had performed. When he used to perform. It had always seemed important.

There were few decorations, nothing to distract him. The rest of the house was covered in pictures, in paintings and photos and sketches. Not here. Just one small photo of Albert propped on top of the shelf by the door.

The piano stood in the middle of the room.

He walked around it a couple of times, as he always did. He closed his eyes and threw his head back. He breathed deeply, and sat down.

He rested his hands for a moment on the cover before lifting it.

He stared. His hands, always so reliable, began to shake.

The world had ended. His life had ended.

Jake.

Jake stands on the footpath facing his house. His schoolbag is
heavy because of all the library books his mother has finally
remembered he has to take back.
*No, that wasn't right. He hadn't been going to school that day. If he'd
been going to school he would have been there already, for hours.*
Jake stands on the footpath facing his house. The street is quiet
for a Saturday. Because it isn't Saturday. It's Tuesday. It feels like
Saturday to Jake because he's not wearing his school uniform.
He's not going to school.
Why was he not going to school? It wasn't the holidays.
He's not going to school because he has a doctor's appointment
about his foot and then his mum is going to take him to
McDonald's for a sundae. He wonders if she'll let him have one
with a flake.
He is sweating. He is sweating because it is very hot. The sun is
big and bright above him and seems to be soaking him right
through to his bones. Deeper than his bones. He wishes he was
wearing jandals instead of lace-up shoes. His mum doesn't like
him to wear jandals anymore because she likes him to always
wear his orthotics. Jake looks down at his feet and frowns. He
hadn't thought his feet would betray him like this. He'd thought
they were allies.
He wishes his mum would hurry up. She's gone back in to the
house because she forgot to bring –

14

What? What had she forgotten?
She forgot to bring something for the smiling lady that had visited last week. She promised to drop something off to her and she's annoyed about it.
Jake's mum is also annoyed that they have to go to the doctor's at midday. When they've gone before it's always been after school but she couldn't get an appointment with the doctor because the doctor's about to get married and go away, Jake thinks perhaps forever. He thinks that maybe if the doctor gets married and goes away forever he'll be able to stop wearing his orthotics and his mum won't be able to tell him off.
Jake has been waiting for a long time. He thinks perhaps seven hours. He wonders if his mum would notice if he snuck past her upstairs and put on his jandals.
When the ground moves, he isn't scared. It does that a lot and all that happens is his cat will run all over the house really fast. Jake thinks that is pretty funny.
He doesn't expect the house to fall down like it does.

Jake lay still on his bed for a while. He didn't think he was right about it being that hot. He thought he was right about most things, but he didn't think it had been hot that day.

He didn't feel much like going downstairs. On this day two years ago his mum had made waffles with bacon and banana and syrup for breakfast, with a candle sticking out of one of the waffles.

Jake didn't think there would be waffles this morning.

He didn't think there would be waffles any morning.

Delia.

AFTER A WHILE DELIA GLANCED at her watch and swore. She'd been gone longer than she should have, naturally. Until a few years ago Delia had never been late, not once in her life, now it happened all the time. Not that there ever was anything in particular to be on time for now, but she didn't like to be so long away.

As she walked down the street, however, her pace slackened. She couldn't help it. She knew that once she got home, it was unlikely she'd get another chance to go out. There was always so much to do, incidental, unimportant things to do: cups of tea to make, lunch to prepare, washing to fold, all the things your average housewife usually had to do.

She could never go off for too long without worrying that something would go wrong, that her mother would need help and be alone, but being in the house sometimes became intolerable. Resolving that ten extra minutes now would help maintain her equilibrium for the rest of the day, she allowed her pace to slow to a light meander. As she walked, she convinced herself that her mother would probably not get out of bed until she was home in any case.

It was still early enough for the streets to be quiet; there were just a few joggers, the keys in their bum pockets jingling slightly as they ran, and some tired-looking besuited men who probably didn't need to spend as much time at work as they thought.

16

Delia breathed deeply as she went, savouring the bright morning air. Again, she paid little attention to her specific route, veering down streets at random, looking at houses she didn't know. She stopped to look at unusual trees and flowers in people's gardens, and spent a while trying to get a reluctant cat to approach her.

The sky grew ever brighter, the day was warming, the clouds were moving on.

Delia reached a church she didn't know and she suddenly felt disconcerted. She should be nearly home by now, there shouldn't be any churches she didn't know.

She looked around her. She'd been walking in the right direction, she was sure of it, but she suddenly realised that it wasn't just the church – she hadn't recognised anything in ages. She shook her head and pressed on. She must only be a couple of streets away; she'd find herself soon.

Mrs Featherby.

MRS FEATHERBY HAD BOILED THE kettle four times whilst waiting for the police constable to arrive. Although she told herself she wanted to be prepared, she also wanted to avoid being the spectacle she knew she'd become. The kitchen was out of sight of the absent wall.

People were beginning to walk along the footpath and, as she had expected, they were staring. Those walking in pairs stopped and muttered to each other. She saw a few take pictures. She wanted to move out of their sight permanently, to live out the rest of her life in the back of the house, but she was afraid of missing the policeman when he arrived. It wasn't as if he would be able to ring the doorbell, after all. She pursed her lips and moved to the kitchen to boil the kettle once more.

When he did eventually arrive he stood on the footpath for what must have been a full two minutes, staring, saying nothing. He didn't seem to notice Mrs Featherby at all until she stepped out into the garden and said, 'Good morning, Constable.'

She supposed constable was still the correct term to use, although, in all honesty, he didn't look much like her idea of a constable. He was of an age at which, according to Mrs Featherby's ideas, a policeman ought to be married, but he was not wearing a ring. He seemed to be suffering from hay fever or a severe head cold, but he was neglecting to use a handkerchief. He arrived with a sandwich in one hand and continually took bites from it as he talked, inconsistently remembering to swallow.

He introduced himself as PC Grigson, gave a hearty sniff, whistled towards the general vicinity of Mrs Featherby's house and said, 'Not sure what I'm going to be able to do for you, love; it's a builder you're going to need.'

Mrs Featherby felt her brow furrow involuntarily at being called 'love', but she decided not to comment.

'Obviously I shall need a builder to fix it, young man. You are here to tell me how it happened. You are here to find out who is responsible and see that the person, or persons, are brought to justice.'

'Right,' said Grigson, running a wrist under his streaming nose. 'So you think we should be looking for a perpetrator?'

'Naturally I think you should be looking for a perpetrator. There has been a theft. Someone has stolen the front wall of my house. I wish to see that person found and held to account.'

'Only thing is, pet, I just don't see how someone can have stolen a whole wall of a house.'

'No, Constable, I'm sure you do not. No more do I. But I believe part of your job consists of investigating how mysterious occurrences have, in fact, occurred. You must find it out.'

'Right,' he sniffed again. 'Sure. Tell you what, I'm going to give you the name of a builder. He's my ex-wife's cousin, as a matter of fact, but he is actually pretty good anyway, and quite reliable, did my bathroom a few months back, and if I give him a call to let him know you're in need, he'll bump you up the list.' He paused and glanced at the gaping hole in the side of the house. 'And I'll have a look through recent records, see if any similar, ah, thefts have occurred in the area.'

'So what am I to do?'

'Oh, you know. Let us know if you think of any other information. If you remember seeing anyone suspicious hanging around, or if you see someone in the future.'

Mrs Featherby didn't quite know how to point out that none of this was in any way useful to her or other potential victims. She elected not to offer PC Grigson a cup of tea.

The copper gave a final sniff, said a non-committal goodbye, and headed back to his car. Mrs Featherby stood alone in her fractured home, vainly attempting to disregard the whispers and stares of her passing neighbours.

Robert.

WHEN HE CAME DOWN TO the kitchen, Robert found Bonny sitting at the table, studiously drawing on one of the bamboo place mats.

'Dad,' said Bonny, fixing Robert with a serious gaze. 'Can I do something different with my cereal today?'

'What did you have in mind?'

'Well, instead of having just one kind of cereal, can I have cornflakes and coco pops mixed all together?'

'That is an excellent idea, Bonny. I'm going to do the same. Would you like a banana sliced on top of yours?'

'Um, not so much. Can I have a banana just on its own?'

Mara walked into the kitchen as they were eating. She had dressed, but not yet done anything with her hair, which stood out from her head in a wild mane of tawny brown. Robert stood and walked over to her. He twisted his hands into the mass of hair and kissed her.

'Nice of you to wait till you'd showered before doing that, my love,' she said.

'Anything for you.'

'I'm glad you feel that way,' said Mara, concentrating harder than was strictly necessary on the cup of coffee she was pouring. 'I've been asked to go in to see Bonny's teacher this afternoon. Can you come?'

'Do they need both of us?'

'No, they didn't say that, it's just that I'm nervous and I'd rather not go alone. It's the first time I've been called in to see a teacher and I don't know what they want. I'm worried I won't act like enough of a grown up.'

'If it were next week I probably could. I've a lot on at the moment. A few people are away at a conference, you know, and we've taken on a couple of important new clients. You'll be fine. They're used to dealing with children, after all. Or can you move the meeting?'

'Next week something else will come up and you still won't be able to go.'

'You can't be sure of that.'

'I am 87 per cent sure of that . . . 87 and a half. There is always something that needs to be done, and it always needs to be done by you because you're a big girly swot who can't delegate.' She rubbed her eyes and took a sip of her coffee. 'It's fine,' she said. 'I can go alone. It's probably no big deal.'

'You sure?'

'Yes, I'm sure, whatever; your job can't be arranged to suit your convenience. Mine can.'

Robert kissed her.

'Don't think I don't envy you that, by the way.'

'Oh, you've no idea,' said Mara, speaking right into his ear, all low and suggestive. 'I can work naked if I want.'

'Bloody hell, Mara,' Robert muttered back. 'And with that image I have to leave. To go to my office. The land where nakedness is a crime. Why didn't I become a website designer? You lot have it so damn sweet.'

'Please. You couldn't handle it. And you've terrible taste.'

'Ooh, right in the feelings.'

Mara gave a bloodthirsty chuckle and ruffled Robert's hair as she walked past him to the cereal.

Robert grabbed his bag from the lounge and headed for the front door.

'Babe,' Mara called from behind him. Robert turned to see her standing in the hall holding her shirt open.

'Mum, can I have a juice?' Bonny called from the kitchen. Mara poked her tongue out and turned to go back to their daughter.

'Bloody hell,' Robert said again as he turned and stepped out into the world.

Jake.

JAKE TRIED HIS HARDEST NOT to expect waffles when he walked into the kitchen, and it was a good thing he did. His dad was eating cereal standing up, staring into the small, overgrown garden. Jake chewed his lip and crossed to the cupboard to look for bread. There were only two pieces left and one of them was an end. He sighed and immediately regretted it. He hated it when people sighed. His dad never sighed, although you'd think he had plenty of reason to. Jake put the bread in the toaster.

'Good morning,' his dad said while Jake was spreading peanut butter on his toast. Jake wondered if it had taken him that long to notice him, or just that long to remember to say hello.

'Hi,' Jake replied.

'Your teacher says you're doing well at school. I called her last night to ask how things were going, how you were settling in.'

Jake had trouble remembering what it had been like talking to his dad before, but he was pretty sure they'd never had conversations like this. Had they talked about TV? Did they tell each other jokes?

'I guess so,' he said. 'I have a spelling test today.'

'Good,' said his dad. 'That's good.'

Jake tried to think of something sensible to say. 'How's your work?' he settled on with a tiny grimace.

'Oh, fine. It's fine. I should get started for the day, actually.'

Jake watched his dad walk out of the kitchen and head slowly to his office. He wondered if he should have had some kind of funny story from school. He couldn't remember if anything funny had happened there recently.

He sat at the table and finished his toast. His dad had forgotten what day it was. He'd forgotten there was something to celebrate. Jake decided not to mind. He decided to try his hardest not to mind. He washed his dishes and went to his room to get his school bag.

Cassie.

CASSIE DIDN'T NOTICE AT FIRST when her phone started to ring. She didn't hear it. At least, she heard it but it felt remote, even though it was in her pocket and vibrating as well as ringing; it wasn't connected to her. It wasn't until she saw someone staring at her that she realised she was supposed to do something about it. That it was hers.

She pulled out the phone, suddenly thinking that maybe it was Floss, that soon they would be laughing over whatever mix up it was that had meant they weren't yet together.

The photo on the display wasn't Floss.

Cassie stood still and gazed at the phone as it went silent and the picture that stared at her from the screen, her mother, disappeared. Disappointment started at the nape of her neck and trickled slowly down her spine, seeping into her through her skin. She breathed deeply for a moment, blinking hard, and called her mother back.

'Well, well?' her mother asked on answering. 'Did she arrive OK? Are you bringing her here? I thought you were bringing her here. I thought you'd be here a couple of hours ago.'

'Um, she's not here yet,' said Cassie, chewing her lip.

'What? Why not?'

'I don't know. I guess something went wrong. She was delayed, maybe.'

'The flight was delayed?'

'No, the flight arrived. She wasn't on it.'

'Where are you?'

'At the airport still. I'm waiting.'

'For what? Planes from Argentina don't arrive every five minutes, Cass. You'd best come home and find out what's happened.'

'Brazil.'

'What? Yes. What? Come home, love, I've a roast in the oven.'

'I'm going to wait a while, Mum. See if I can find out anything here.'

Cassie's mum was still talking, but a large German tour group was walking past, their voices raised in excitement, and Cassie couldn't hear her anymore. She hung up and slipped her phone back into her pocket.

The crowd surged around her, pushing at her, catching her hair in the zips of their bags, but she did not move.

She didn't realise it, but she had not moved in five hours.

Delia.

DELIA'S SHOULDER WAS ACHING FROM carrying her bag. Why
had she even brought it? It felt like she'd packed for a weekend
away, instead of a light stroll and a read. She'd been walking for
over an hour and she had no idea where she was. She couldn't
figure out how she could have got lost. She never did pay much
attention to where she was going, but then she'd never really needed
to. She always found her way.

She pulled out her phone, feeling stupid for needing it, and
brought up her little blue dot. There she was, standing on a street.
She could see the street she wanted; it was much further away
than she'd realised. She'd bypassed her neighbourhood completely
and veered off wildly to the north. She checked which direction
she needed to walk in and set off purposefully down the road.

It was five minutes before she realised she'd gone in the wrong
direction. She checked the map, and tried again.

She could see clearly where she needed to go, but every time
she looked up and started moving, she lost sight of it. She tried
holding her phone in front of her face, but even then it didn't
seem to relate. No matter what she tried she ended up walking
further away.

Delia decided to find the nearest bus stop and get home from
there. After giving up on her phone, she walked, even more
purposefully, for another ten minutes. The street she was on was
tiny and winding. She stopped for a moment, wondering if it was

best to go back the way she'd come or continue on in the same direction. She couldn't remember seeing a bus stop recently so there had to be one coming up.

She kept walking. The area was small and residential and void of transport links. Each winding road, flanked by brick houses, led to another, more winding road, flanked by more brick houses.

The sun had returned in full force and Delia's back was itchy with sweat.

After a further twenty-five minutes, Delia heard what she was certain was a lorry. It didn't sound far away; it was somewhere ahead of her. She picked up the pace, her eyes set forwards, weary and desperate, and the street soon broke out into a small row of shops with, oh joy, a bus stop.

After a few minutes, a bus pulled up and a weary Delia hopped onto it. A whimper rose up within her, but she remembered she was in public for long enough to quell it. She flung herself into a seat and closed her eyes. She had no idea how she'd managed to go so far astray. She leant forward with her head in her hands as the bus trundled her towards home.

Robert.

ROBERT FOUGHT HIS WAY THROUGH the crowd of commuters to exit the tube station. He climbed the escalators with more of a wince than usual, regretting the morning's ill-advised run. He should do that more often, he thought. Or never again. As always, he got out a stop early to get a bit of air before being confined at his desk all day. As he walked, his mind was still at home with Mara and Bonny. He knew the day would be long, he knew he'd be tired and moody by the end of it, he wished he could have just called in sick. He hadn't faked a sick day since he was fifteen though; he'd almost forgotten how to do it. He sighed as he turned onto his street, thinking about what he and Mara could be doing if he didn't have a responsible job.

He'd gone two blocks too far before he noticed he'd passed his building. He turned back, still smirking, and walked three blocks too far in the other direction. He stopped and tried to concentrate. He walked directly and purposely to the position of his office. He didn't get there. He paused and looked around. This time he'd made it to roughly the right position on the road, but for some reason he wasn't at his building. In fact, he couldn't see his building at all.

Suddenly he chuckled. He was clearly on the wrong street. He retraced his steps back a couple of blocks. He was sure he was on the right track now. He turned down the street he'd turned down every weekday morning and quite a few Saturdays for the last six and a half years. How had he got this wrong? He strode on.

He stopped. He'd gone too far again. No, he hadn't, he'd not gone far enough.

No. No, that wasn't it at all.

He was in the right place, he was in the exact spot, but there was no work. His work wasn't there.

The entire building was gone, vanished as if it had never been there at all.

Robert turned around slowly, twice. There was the travel agent he'd booked his and Mara's last holiday in. There was the French restaurant that used to be really great but had then changed hands and gone sharply downhill. There was the hotel that seemed a bit rugged but that Robert had once seen a quite famous actor he could never remember the name of leaving. There was the new building that housed three identical nondescript businesses with shiny receptions and ambiguous names. Robert's building should have been next to the hotel, but it wasn't.

Robert stood staring at the lack of his work for ten minutes, with no idea what to do. His body was frozen while his mind tried and failed to comprehend the vanishing of the building that should have been right in front of him.

Marcus.

HE SPENT TWO HOURS STARING at his piano before he could think clearly enough to do anything. He would have to call her. He didn't want to worry her, but he didn't know what to do. He couldn't deal with it alone. He went to the phone in the kitchen.

The phone rang five times and her voice came on: 'Hi hi, Katy here, I'm obviously busy. Leave a message if you want.'

He hung up and immediately dialled again. On his fourth attempt it was answered by a gruff-sounding male.

''Lo?'

'Hello. May I speak with Katharine?'

'Um, yeah, all right. Who's it?'

'It's her father.'

'Oh, right! Hiya Marcus, it's Jasper.'

He'd forgotten there was a new boy. 'Oh. Hello Jasper.' There was a brief pause.

'I'll get Kate, then, yeah?'

'Thank you.'

He waited, listening to his daughter and her lover exchange the phone.

'Dad? What's up?'

'They're gone. My keys. Gone.'

'You can't find your keys? Do you need to go out somewhere? I'm sure it'll be OK; you've a quiet neighbourhood. Ask your neighbour, that lovely woman with all the hair, to keep an eye out.'

'No, no. Not the house keys. The other keys. My keys. My piano keys.'

There was a pause.

'Dad? Dad, are you all right?'

'Of course I'm not all right. I need to play. I need to play my piano and my piano keys are gone.'

There was a long pause on the phone. He stood still and waited for her to talk.

'Dad,' she said eventually. 'I don't, I mean, they can't be.'

'How am I supposed to play?'

'How can they just be missing?'

'Don't know,' he said. 'Just are.'

'OK.' She paused for a moment. 'It'll be fine, Dad. I'm coming over. We'll sort this out.'

'Right.' He hung up and walked back towards the music room. He stood in the door. Couldn't bear to go further. Two or three more steps and he'd be able to see it. He didn't want to see it. He couldn't see it. Not again. Not alone. He would wait.

Delia.

'Mum!' Delia called as she staggered in through the front door after a twenty-five-minute bus ride. 'I'm sorry! Are you OK?'

'I'm fine, of course, Dee, darling, but where have you been?' Delia's mum wheeled herself through from the living room, appearing to be more curious than worried or distressed.

'Sorry. I suppose I got lost. Are you hungry?'

'Oh yes. I've had a banana, but it's not quite, you know. . . It's not like you to get lost, Dee. I don't think you ever have before.'

Delia followed her mother into the kitchen and began making them both breakfast.

'I know,' she said. 'I don't know what happened. It's a lovely day out there now, though. Maybe we should go for a walk later. We could have a picnic.'

'Oh. Perhaps. It's just, well, I've gotten to a rather exciting point in the Willow Tree Sampler and I want to keep going.'

'We could bring that with us, though, Mum.' Delia tried not to sound as if she was pleading. 'You could work on it in the park.'

'Oh no. No, the wind could pick up and wreak havoc with the cotton. It's far too risky. Let's have a nice day indoors. You can read or play on your computer and I'll work on the sampler and we can have cups of tea whenever we want.'

Jake.

JAKE STOOD ALONE IN THE corridor, frowning at the wall. He had been lying all day. He'd lied to his class. His teacher had asked him if it was a special day for him, using that extra-chirpy voice she had sometimes, as if she was winking with her entire head, and he'd lied and said no. He'd said there must be a mistake on the register.

He didn't know why he'd lied. It *was* a special day for him. He wanted it to be special. He wanted to be sung to, but he'd lied and said no, and no one had sung.

There was a clip clopping of shoes behind him and Jake turned around.

'Mr Baxter, school finished fifteen minutes ago. I'm sure someone's waiting outside to collect you.'

She wasn't Jake's teacher so he didn't know her name. He thought she maybe taught in the room next to his or the one next to that. She was looking at him the way adults always did: as though unsure of how to talk to him, as though they didn't know if he could hear their words, and they wanted to make extra sure he understood what they were saying. They looked in his eyes a lot, all the adults.

She was wrong, there would be no one to collect him. Of course there wouldn't; Jake had been walking to school by himself for ages. Ever since they'd moved here and school had been close enough to walk to. If someone had been collecting him, it would have to be his dad, and if his dad was collecting him, he'd be late or he'd forget. Jake didn't know if his dad would have been late if he'd had to pick him up in the old days, but he knew he'd be late now.

Jake said nothing and walked slowly towards the doors.

It was usually only a ten-minute walk to Jake's house, but Jake stretched it out to almost twenty.

He could tell his dad was in his office, but he didn't go in. Instead he went to the kitchen. He opened the cupboards and looked inside. Then he looked in the fridge. There were no special foods. There was no cake. There was no fizzy drink. There were no lollies.

It was Jake's birthday and no one knew.

Jake wondered if it would be better if he didn't know himself. Part of him wanted to never have another birthday at all.

Jake's last birthday had been the worst day ever. The second-worst day ever. No one had known how to celebrate it. No one had really wanted to celebrate it anyway. Jake hadn't. Last year he'd felt as if he'd never wanted to celebrate anything ever again. His mum had always made amazing food. Jake hadn't wanted anyone trying to make food as good as his mum's food.

This year, though, he wanted something to happen. He didn't really mind what it was. He didn't mind if someone tried to make amazing food and it actually turned out to be quite bad food. He just wanted them to try. He just wanted it to still be important to someone that he was having a birthday.

Mrs Featherby.

THE BUILDER, WHO'D INTRODUCED HIMSELF simply as Bruno, sucked air through his teeth and looked at Mrs Featherby's absence of wall speculatively.

'Well,' said Mrs Featherby. 'How soon can you have a wall for me?'

'Christ,' he said, as if that was a sufficient answer. He walked across Mrs Featherby's yard with callous disregard for her roses, and he gazed in at her exposed rooms. Mrs Featherby was glad to see her roses put up a bit of a fight, in the form of a thorn snagging on the corner of the man's t-shirt as he passed, pulling a thread loose.

'I mean, holy shit, you know,' he continued. Mrs Featherby did not deign to reply. She waited, arms crossed low on her hips, one brogued foot resisting the urge to tap impatiently. She reminded herself that she ought to be grateful for the builder's quick arrival, grateful she'd not had to wait until tomorrow.

'It's not going to be easy,' he said. 'It's not going to be quick. I mean, I've never even seen this happen. How did this happen?'

'I have put the police in charge of ascertaining that.'

Bruno scoffed lightly.

Mrs Featherby suddenly found him a much more sympathetic character; she felt an unexpected urge to give an answering smirk. 'How long?' she asked. 'How long will it take? When will you have a wall for me?'

'Well, it's not like I can just order in one wall, please, and slot it into place. I have to match the materials; I have to integrate what I do with the existing house, which, by the way, is over 150 years old. And the other walls are plaster over brick, which I can do, or I can put up a dry wall and then just put bricks over the outside.'

'But that wouldn't be the same as the rest of the house. It wouldn't be the same as it was.'

'No. But it would be easier for you. There would be something up to protect you.'

'Please rebuild it as it was. Keep it the same.'

'Well, it's up to you,' said the builder.

'How long will it be?'

'Hard to say. I'll have to find the exact brick, or as close as I can, so I'll need to call a few people before I can say. I don't like to give an estimate, you know, and then have it take longer.'

'I appreciate that, young man, but I have to live here. This is my home. You may think you have a problem of an old house that's missing a wall; I have a problem that my home is broken.'

'You might want to think about where else you can stay. You got family or friends that'd put you up? That's what you're going to need to do.'

'That's not possible,' said Mrs Featherby cooly. 'Nor am I willing to stay in a hotel. This is my home and I do not wish to leave it.'

'Well. I guess, if you're sure. The most I can do for now is rig up some kind of temporary protection for you. Something to keep the weather outside. Bloody lucky it's still warm. No telling how long that'll last, mind.'

'Indeed.'

Mrs Featherby tried to get on with her day while the builder attached a thick sheet of plastic to the gaping side of the house. She baked a chocolate cake and darned a batch of old socks. She laundered the guest linens she kept, in spite of the fact that she never had any guests.

Finally, after the builder was done, he gave Mrs Featherby a sympathetic nod as he went to leave.

'Not sure what this'll end up costing. If you put me in touch with your insurance company I can deal with it all directly with them. Save you some stress, right?'

'Thank you. I shall call them directly and let them have your number.'

Mrs Featherby gave Bruno the builder a slice of cake and sent him on his way.

Cassie.

CASSIE HAD ALMOST STOPPED SEEING her surroundings. Her eyelids drooped and flickered, and although her gaze was still fixed on the arrivals gate, she was having trouble differentiating between the people who walked through it.

She was just becoming aware of an ache in her neck when a woman walked up to her and put a hand on her shoulder.

'Cass?'

Cassie gave a start and blinked a couple of times.

'Oh, Mum. You didn't have to come all the way out here.'

'You stopped answering your phone. I was worried.'

'No, I'm fine. I'm just waiting. I'll wait here.'

'Cass, I think you should come home.'

Cassie was so tired. Too tired to argue really, but she didn't want to give in. She bit her lip and stared stubbornly at the gate.

'It's going to get late, love. You've been here for hours. Come home and we'll figure out what's happened. Maybe she's going to come tomorrow. You can come back tomorrow. I'll come with you.'

Cassie swallowed.

'You must be hungry, Cass. There's dinner at home. I did a crumble.'

Cassie breathed in deeply and closed her eyes.

'Come on. We'll sort it out in the morning.'

Cassie sighed and took her mother's arm. 'I can't move,' she said. 'I can't move my feet.'

They both looked down at Cassie's feet. The brown leather of her sandals had become rough as bark. Her skin had merged with them and her toes had put forth roots into the floor. She was growing into the ground.

Robert.

AFTER A WHILE ROBERT DECIDED to call his assistant. Assistants were supposed to always know what was going on, so Derek would know. It was Derek's job to know. He pulled out his phone and scrolled through his contact list. He was halfway through the Fs before he realised he'd gone too far. He scrolled back up. Derek's name wasn't there. This was obviously ridiculous, it had been there yesterday; he'd hardly have deleted it. You don't delete your assistant's number, otherwise how can you call him when you've sent him out somewhere and tell him to bring you back an almond croissant? You can't. He looked again. There was no Derek. Derek was gone. Feverishly, he scrolled through the names on his phone, looking for his boss, his intern, the receptionist, but none of them were there. His colleagues were gone. Work was gone. Everything was gone.

Robert walked back down the street in a daze. He wandered past buildings that had not disappeared, through crowds of people who would manage to arrive at their destinations. He didn't stop until he reached the river. He sat on a bench and stared in front of him.

Slowly the foot traffic that passed him changed from harried business people into slowly meandering tourists. A young couple approached him and asked for directions.

'I told you,' the girl said, elbowing the boy in the ribs. 'You should always listen to me.'

'OK, OK,' the boy said. 'I mean, I'm sure you're right about that, maybe, but I'm probably not going to.'

Robert stared after them as they walked away. He got out his phone and stared at it, suddenly frightened. Derek had vanished from it, what if Mara had too? What if he'd go home to find his house had vanished as well, and Mara and Bonny with it? Robert once again scrolled through the contacts list on his phone. Mara. There she was. Mara. His torchbearer.

He called her but it went to voicemail. Of course it did, he thought, he ought to have known better; she hated being interrupted, she would have left her phone upstairs where it wouldn't distract her.

Robert sat and stared at the Thames. He got up and walked along it and sat on another bench. He crossed over and walked back up the other side. He browsed the gift shops of the theatres and art galleries. He sat at a rickety table outside and drank a burnt coffee. He walked over to the river again and stared down into its muddy dullness. He wandered away.

It wasn't until a few hours later that he came across a tube station and decided to go home.

Marcus.

THE DOOR OPENING STARTLED HIM. He had no idea how much time had passed.

'Dad?'

She looked like her mother. Funny how a girl raised by two men can so closely resemble the mother she barely knew. Not that 'mother' was really the right word. But then, what was? Nothing. There was no right word.

'Don't you have a class?'

'Jasper's taking notes for me. I was worried.'

'I don't know what to do.'

She blinked at him and walked into the room. She crossed to the piano and opened the cover.

'Oh my god.'

'What?'

'They're really gone.'

He'd been hoping he was crazy.

'What did you do with them?' she asked.

'Me? I didn't touch them. Not since yesterday. Not since I was playing yesterday. They were fine.'

'So, they just vanished?'

'Yes. I came down this morning, I had my breakfast, I went to play. They were gone.'

She stared. She wrinkled her nose. No, she didn't look like her mother. She looked like Albert. Thank god.

She hesitantly put out a hand as if to touch the keys that weren't there, then abruptly shut the lid.

'Let's have a cup of tea,' she said. 'I went to Fortnum's and got some new ones for us to try.'

She walked out of the room, giving Albert's picture a casual pat as she passed it, and led the way into the kitchen.

'I thought we could all have dinner tonight,' she said, pulling down a tea pot. 'I asked Jasper to come over and bring some food from the Iraqi place around the corner. That's the place that we got the really good fish from that time, isn't it? And you haven't really spent any time with Jasper; haven't you only met him the once? It's my fault, of course. I should have brought him around here earlier.'

She stopped pottering around and sat at the table across from him.

'What do I do?'

'I don't know, Dad. I suppose I'll call a piano repair company. Do you think it'd cost a lot to replace them?'

The question unsettled him. It was his piano. He didn't want someone else's hands on his piano.

He suddenly didn't like being still. He took his cup to the sink even though it wasn't yet even half empty. He couldn't decide if he wanted to empty it or keep drinking.

'Dad?'

'When's he, when's he coming? Your boy?'

'It's OK. I don't have to ring someone now. We'll just take some time. We won't think about it for a while.'

His arm was itchy. Something had bitten him.

'Dad?'

He turned back.

'Right. Yes. Dinner will be lovely. We'll have dinner.'

Delia.

DELIA LAY IN BED THAT night, still embarrassed about how wildly she'd got lost. There weren't all that many things she prided herself on these days, but her unerring sense of direction was one of them, and it was something she needed.

Most of her days were spent in the same way, in the same place. She'd grown to rely on being able to escape, to wander in any direction for as long as she needed to, being fully confident that she'd have no trouble finding her way back when she needed to. Admitting to this tiny failure was somehow more difficult than admitting to all the giant ones.

Although she wasn't yet aware of it, and would never fully figure it out, a very specific thing was happening to Delia, and had been happening for years. The morning's unwanted adventure was nothing more than the latest in a slow decline that had been precipitated by a small van full of tea and biscuits running a red light when Delia was 147 words away from finishing her dissertation.

Those 147 words had never been written.

Mrs Featherby.

'YOUR WHAT'S BEEN STOLEN?' said the brisk voice on the phone. It was several notes higher in tone than it had been thirty seconds previously. The bored indifference was almost entirely gone.

'My wall,' replied Mrs Featherby, patiently and efficiently. 'The front wall of my house.'

'Bloody hell, how did that happen?'

'I don't know how. I've reported it to the police. I'm sure they'll have some kind of answer shortly.' Mrs Featherby was not at all convinced that the police were going to come up with any kind of solution, but it would not do to express doubt to the insurance agent. Insurance agents pounce on doubt like rabid terriers. They could probably smell it, the way dogs can smell fear.

'To be honest, Mrs, I'm not sure about this. I'm not sure about it at all.'

'My home and contents insurance covers me against theft, does it not?'

'Well, yeah, sure, but that's theft of, well, the contents. Not theft of the house.'

'The house has not been stolen. Only part of it has.'

'Yeah, I know, but—'

'If an unruly university student uplifted my mail box or my rose bush or my door knocker, which is an antique in the shape of an elephant, would that be covered?'

'I suppose—'

'Well, this is precisely the same situation. Someone has stolen from me; they've stolen a part of my house, including, I might add, my front door and, by extension, my rather lovely door knocker.'

The insurance agent changed tack: 'Yeah, well, we can't even know for sure that it's theft, can we? Your wall disappearing. Can't be that common, wall thieves. And you're not covered for acts of God, so—'

'Acts of God?' said Mrs Featherby, audibly raising her eyebrow. 'Are you actually suggesting that our Lord and Saviour, in His infinite wisdom, has used His omnipotent power to cause my front wall to dissolve away? Balaam had his donkey, Joan had her magic voices and I have a disappearing house? Is that, in your mind, the most logical explanation?'

'Look, there's no need—'

'Perhaps you would be so good as to allow me to put in a claim, and if in the processing of that claim it is decided that the theft of my wall was, in fact, not theft but the divine intervention of the Almighty, you can take the moral high ground.'

There was a brief silence.

'Could you confirm your post code, please?'

Robert.

ROBERT ARRIVED HOME JUST AS Mara and Bonny were getting out of the car.

'Dad!' said Bonny. 'Did you know that lions can't purr and we get to have pizza for dinner even though it's not a Friday or a birthday? But not shop pizza; Mum's going to make it. I would be sad if I were a lion that couldn't purr. I wish humans could purr.'

'You're home early and oh my god, you're not going to believe it,' said Mara.

'What?' said Robert.

'Just, just wait. A bit. Bonny, do you want to play a game while your dad and I cook dinner?'

'Can dad not play with me?'

'Not this time, pal,' said Robert, staring curiously at Mara.

'So,' she said once she and Robert were alone in the kitchen. 'So, I may have pulled her out of school.'

'What?' said Robert. 'Why? Where are we going to send her?'

'I know, oh I know, but honestly, I can't even—'

'Jeepers, Mara, breathe.'

Mara closed her mouth and glared at him.

'Just, what happened, OK?'

'All right. So, I get there, and everyone's acting super nice, you know, would you like tea and a biscuit, like the school is a little old woman luring you into her house before she bakes you into a pie.'

'I think she'd probably get more than one pie out of a whole human.'

'And then they sit you down and start talking and it seems like they're being nice, but halfway through you think, "hold on, you think I'm a idiot" and "fuck right off", but you don't want to interrupt them, because you've a mouth full of tea-dunked biscuit and it's just not necessary to show people the inside of your mouth when it's all coated in brown.'

'But what did they say?'

Mara sighed and leaned forward with her elbows on the bench and her face in her hands.

'OK, OK. So, apparently, a few weeks ago, when they took the register, instead of saying "present" like all the other children, Bonny got up, climbed onto her chair, and sang "Go Your Own Way".'

'Great song.'

'And I mean, she didn't just sing the chorus, she sang the whole song.'

'Well, it's not long, once you've taken out all the guitar solos. Unless she sang those too.'

'I didn't ask. Anyway, the next day it was "Short People".'

'Hey, that's our song. She and I play it together. Well, I play the actual song and she plays a rather Dadaist solo. And sings, obviously.'

'Well, her teacher's only five foot tall, so I doubt it went down particularly well.'

'That's a bit rude of her; she's still much taller than Bonny.'

'Next it was "The Only Living Boy in New York".'

'Ooh, she's been listening to your music.'

'After a week or so, the other children started copying her.'

'Typical. That's exactly how indie trends become mainstream.'

'Apparently it now takes an average of an hour and twenty minutes to take the register.'

'Yeah, but it's an hour and twenty minutes of pure joy. Well, assuming the other children are OK at carrying a tune.'

'I think they're more worried about cutting into valuable learning time. Anyway, they told her she couldn't sing in class and she asked them why and they said because class wasn't an appropriate place to sing and she asked them why not and obviously they'd started a never-ending discussion, because she's a child, isn't she, so they tried to cut it short by saying that if she ever answered the register with a song again she'd have to stay in for playtime and she wouldn't be allowed to read or play with the toys, and she just cried and cried and all the other children cried, so they asked me if we would punish her at home for doing it so they don't have to punish her at school and make all the children cry.'

'Bloody hell. Bloody hell! They were going to . . . a school was going to tell a child she wasn't allowed to read? Because she sings, she's not allowed to read?'

'I'm not telling her she can't stand on a chair and sing, Rob. I'm not ever telling her that.'

Robert put a hand on the back of Mara's neck and began massaging the base of her head.

'I think we shouldn't start off by letting her have a holiday.'

'No. I think you're right. I guess I'll home-school her until we've found somewhere else.'

'How will you meet your deadlines?'

'I'll have to work that out, won't I? I don't have anything due till the middle of next week.'

'We have the best kid, Mara.'

'The best.'

She sighed and pulled out the chopping board.

'How was your day?'

'Oh,' said Robert. 'Fine. You know. Nothing as dramatic as this.'

The day no longer seemed real to him. The impossibility of his work having actually vanished was far more real than his memory of it having done so. He wondered if he'd imagined it. He'd go back to work the next day and it would all be as normal.

51

Jake.

JAKE SAT AT THE KITCHEN table and did his homework without being asked. He started reading a book his teacher had said was good. His dad came in and looked in the cupboards. He looked in the fridge. He took out the leftover chicken from the night before and made soup. He defrosted bread rolls. He asked Jake about school and nodded as Jake talked. They went to the living room and silently watched some reality TV.

Jake blinked a couple of times as he looked at his dad. He seemed unclear, almost blurred. It was as if Jake was looking at him through a faint mist.

When Jake went to bed there was a card on his pillow. It had a picture of Spider-Man on it. Inside, below the printed message, it said, 'Love you. Sorry. Dad.'

Cassie.

CASSIE WAS EXHAUSTED. THE TIDE of people that had surged around her after the discovery of her roots had baffled and broken her.

Her mother's panicked screams had first brought security running. Then there had been medics, and a call over the loudspeaker for a doctor that resulted only in a seething crowd of curious onlookers.

All attempts to prise Cassie out of the floor had failed. The roots that her feet had become looked small, but they were strong and seemed to run deep. It wasn't until Cassie was shaking with hysteria that someone saw fit to move the people on. They had brought some screens, like the kind you see in hospitals, and placed them around Cassie so she was protected from the curious stares. Cassie had forbidden her mother from spending the night behind the screens with her, but she was sure she was somewhere around. The nearest chair, probably.

The relief at being alone, or at least feeling alone, was dizzying. The freedom to think hit her like a drug. There was one thought that she had been frantic to return to: where was Floss? Cassie had checked the flight details until she had them by heart, and then gone on checking them. She couldn't have been wrong.

And Floss must have been on the plane. If she had missed it, there were hours in which she could have let Cassie know what had gone wrong and how it was being fixed. She had been coming. She had been coming to Cassie.

Cassie didn't doubt Floss's intent to be there. Floss loved her. Floss would do anything to be there. It was not possible that Cassie could love Floss with so much of herself and Floss not love her back. It was not possible that the tether connecting Cassie to Floss went only in one direction.

Floss was coming. She was coming and Cassie was determined to be waiting for her.

The Status.

ONCE UPON A TIME, GEORGE Fortescue had status. Until one day, he lost it.

He had always been the kind to turn heads. Not because he was particularly good looking, he wasn't. Not because he was tall, he was average. There was simply something about him. At school he'd been listened to by his peers. When he gave answers in class, the other students were silent. No one ever made fun of him, not because they were afraid of him, or liked him particularly, but because somehow the idea of making fun of George was too remote to consider. When he started work he was quickly promoted, although his work was not noticeably better than anyone else's. He was marked out for leadership from the start; without talent, or charisma, he had status.

And then he didn't. He himself didn't realise that he'd lost it. But all of a sudden people were slower to make way for him in the street. His success rate at hailing cabs went down by 40 per cent overnight. The board of directors took no note of his opinions. His staff started whispering behind his back, nothing he wanted done got done.

A few months later he would retire and move to Cornwall. He would get a cat on the misplaced assumption that it, at least, would show him some respect.

The Fight.

WILL GOWAN AND JEFF BROWN lost a fight. Both boys knew where it was when they left their respective houses. They walked confidently towards it, flanked by their gangs. They met a block away from the fight's last known location, but pretended not to notice each other. Their gangs didn't pretend not to notice each other, they scowled and glowered for all they were worth.

Two crowds of boys headed down opposite sides of the street until they reached the same corner, the corner around which the fight was.

It wasn't there.

For the first time, the leaders looked at each other.

'Where is it?' said Will.

'Have we lost it?' said Jeff.

'We can't both have lost it,' said Will.

But they had.

The Looks.

WINIFRED GRAHAM LOST HER LOOKS. She hunted for them carefully and methodically, but they were all gone. It seemed remarkable for them to have all disappeared at once, but although she tried, she could not find a single one.

Her looks had been so many. So many looks, and they were glorious: a look to show a secret, a look to freeze blood, one to curdle milk, a look of longing, a look of rejection, a look of despair. A look of love.

It would be several weeks before she managed to leave her house. To confront a world in which she would now have to rely on words.

The Heart.

AND BARNABY JONES LOST HIS heart. He was fifty-seven years old and had kept a good handle on it until that day. He'd never had to question its whereabouts at school or university, even when his friends were finding theirs so hard to keep track of. He'd checked for its presence as he left the house each morning, along with his keys and wallet. There was a brief moment in his mid-thirties when he couldn't remember where he'd left it, but a quick search revealed not far from its usual place.

Then this day, seven weeks before his 58th birthday, it was gone. After searching his house thoroughly and to no avail, he retraced his steps, eventually coming across the finder of his heart. Unfortunately he would be unable to get it back from her, and before he would have time to think of staying near her, just so as to always be near his heart, she would not have it anymore.

From then, Barnaby's heart would change hands with dizzying frequency. He would do his best to keep up with it, but it would show itself determined to evade him. Try as he might to get it back, in the end he would have to learn to do without it.

Jake.

Jake stands on the footpath facing his house. The street is quiet, because it is not Saturday. Even though it's Tuesday, Jake is not wearing his uniform. Not wearing his school uniform on a Tuesday that's not in the holidays makes Jake feel like he's breaking the rules. But he can't get into trouble because his mum is the one who's told him not to wear it.

Jake doesn't want to go to the doctor. The doctor is boring and he doesn't like someone looking at his feet that closely. He doesn't want to go to the doctor, but he does want to go to McDonald's.

He is not wearing a jersey, but he should be. The day is cold; the first cold day in ages and Jake isn't prepared for it. His mum said that he should put on a jumper, but he didn't. He looks down at the goosebumps on his arm and wishes his mum would hurry up.

She's gone back into the house because she forgot to bring a recipe she'd promised to drop off to the smiling lady that sometimes comes over with her friend Mel. Jake knows his mum doesn't like the smiling lady, because she never uses her name. She always just calls her Goldilocks, which is not a real name at all. Jake doesn't know what the smiling lady's real name is.

Jake can tell his mum is really grumpy because she's already dropped her keys on the floor three times. Jake's mum is always clumsy when she's cross. When she'd turned to go back into the house, Jake had started to go with her and she'd snapped at him to stay where he was and wait for her. Jake's mum hardly ever snaps.

Jake has been waiting for a long time.

The ground moves like it does a lot. Like it never used to. It started happening a few months ago, after that one big time when buildings came down. Jake was scared when it started, when it happened months ago, but he isn't anymore. It doesn't really make anything happen.

This time, though, something does. This time something awful happens.

Jake looked down at his arm. There were goosebumps on it now. Had there been that day? He didn't think so. He couldn't remember feeling cold, but he couldn't remember not feeling cold either. He couldn't be sure.

He so wanted to be sure.

He trudged slowly along the road towards his house. Without really planning to, he kept walking past it and around the corner. He wandered until he was on a street he didn't know, walking along a row of shops. Also without planning to, Jake stopped walking. He looked around himself, up and down the quiet street.

The shop he was standing outside didn't seem to have a name. He stood looking for several minutes but there wasn't one anywhere. There was the street number, hand-painted in pea green, and that was all except for a small blackboard hanging on the door which read, 'Nothing can be found that is not lost'. Jake wasn't sure he knew what that meant.

He pushed open the door and walked in. The shop was dark inside, and dusty, and full of second-hand things. There was a shelf of old typewriters by the door, and a pile of battered books stacked precariously on top of a rusty umbrella stand.

'Shouldn't you be in school?' said a voice from the ether.

'Yes.' Jake blinked and peered around the shop, trying to locate the speaker.

The Voice was sitting in an armchair in the corner. She had her legs slung over one arm of the chair and a book in her lap. She watched Jake for a while as he looked around.

'Well?' she said eventually. 'Buying or selling?'

'What?'

The Voice got up from her armchair and leaned over the shop counter towards Jake.

'Are you buying or are you selling?'

'I don't have anything to sell.'

'Well, wouldn't you suppose that that means you're buying?'

Jake fingered the money in his pocket. His dad had left it on the table and probably forgotten about it. They had run out of milk and bread. His dad had probably forgotten about that too.

'Yes,' he said. 'I'm buying.'

'What are you looking for?'

'Something interesting.'

'Everything's interesting.'

Jake's wandering gaze fell on a small, silvery, old mirror.

'Who's was that?'

The Voice followed Jake's eyes, shook her head and leaned further forward, with a conspiratorial air. 'That,' she began dramatically, 'belonged to a war heroine. She came from a small village near Cambridge, and when things started to turn to custard over the way, she ran off to Paris and joined the French Resistance. She carried that mirror with her always, to make sure her hair was in place while she fought the Nazis. Then, when she died, her granddaughter, who is the kind of person who is Not Interested, inherited it. She brought it here to sell because she thought it was tacky.'

Jake picked up a pair of cufflinks from a shelf.

'Those,' said The Voice, 'were sold to me by the new husband of their owner's wife. She had asked him to return them to her ex-husband, but he was so jealous he couldn't stand to see him. So he brought them to me instead.'

Jake put the cufflinks back and turned to a pile of books. The one on the top was small and red and faded. He opened the cover and read the inscription: 'You are the reason I'm glad there are words.'

'Who's was this?' he asked The Voice.

'Oh, I don't actually know about that. Some woman found it when she moved into a new house. It had fallen behind a radiator or something.'

'I'll buy this, I think,' said Jake. 'What was the woman like?' he asked as The Voice counted out his change. 'Tall. A bit chub. Had a baby. Very, very long hair. Blonde.'

'When did she sell you the book?'

'Holy hell, I don't know. A month ago maybe. Maybe two.'

'Great,' said Jake. 'Thanks. I'll see you.'

Jake could feel The Voice staring after him as he left the shop.

He walked the three blocks to his house as quickly as he could. He was feeling sort of fevered, but he didn't know why. He let himself into the house. The door to his dad's office was open, and Jake could tell he was in there, but he didn't go in, nor did his dad come out to see who had come in, or to ask Jake why he wasn't at school.

Jake climbed the stairs to his room and shut the door behind him. It was no good. There was too much stuff, too much clutter. His mum used to make him tidy his room all the time but now no one did. Jake hadn't noticed how messy it had become. He put the small red book carefully on his pillow and began to tidy. He folded his clothes and put them in his drawers. He slipped his books neatly onto their shelves.

When everything had been put away and the floor was clear, he took the red book and placed it in the middle of the floor. He took a piece of paper and wrote, 'Book. Gift. Behind radiator.' He put the paper beside the book. He leaned back against his bed and looked at it.

Delia.

THERE WAS A ROOM IN Delia's house that Delia never went into. It had been her room when she was a child, and for all her trips home after she moved away to study.

It was still decorated in the style she'd chosen when she was thirteen. Redecoration had been her birthday present that year and she'd spent hours deciding on and second-guessing colour choices. Three of the walls (luscious cherry 037) were almost entirely obscured by posters of pop singers and movie stars, many of which had come unstuck in key top corners. The fourth wall (bruised concrete 109) had a series of doodles in white paint that had started as a rebellion and grown into a meandering, wordless story. The curtains (dark purple brocade) had been closed for years. The bed (single, patchwork mainly in pink) was unmade. The last time Delia had slept in it had been the Easter holidays, a few weeks before the accident that would bring her home for good. She was supposed to wash the sheets and remake the bed herself, having never officially lifted the Keep Out Agreement of 97, but she'd been late for her train and had left them.

But it wasn't the garishly twee decor or the depressing insight into adolescent Delia's psyche that kept grown-up Delia out of the room.

When Delia had moved back home, she'd taken the seven boxes marked 'Master's Degree' and stacked them in the middle of the room. She'd piled sketches and paintings on the bed, she'd dumped her easel, her box of paints and brushes, and her blank canvases on the floor and closed the door on them. She'd taken over the room that her mother would no longer be able to use.

If Delia had gone into that room, if she'd unpacked the boxes marked 'Master's Degree', and if she'd gone further and unpacked 'Bachelor's Degree' and 'College' and 'Secondary School', and even 'Primary School', she would have looked over a startlingly consistent academic history.

'Delia is a quiet and driven child,' Miss Gooding had probably written twenty years earlier. 'She shows extraordinary focus and is progressing well. She is reading well above her age level, and has shown marked improvement in maths, despite her tendency to doodle all over her work.'

Ten years after that, Mr Brown might have said Delia was 'A solid A-plus student who clearly prioritises her studies above all else. She is very goal-oriented and works unceasingly to achieve her high aims. She has clear artistic talent, which she has worked hard at developing.'

It's likely that her university essays and portfolios carried barely legible statements like, 'Your continued efforts to extend yourself are clearly evident and, once again, you've met with success.'

There may have been a side note on an essay she'd never collected that read 'I look forward to your dissertation and final project.'

But Delia never did go into that room. She never did unpack her many boxes. She didn't look at her half-finished paintings or read over her old art history books. She went for walks to nowhere. She came home. She slept. And repeat.

Marcus.

DIDN'T SEEM TO BE MUCH point in getting out of bed. Didn't seem like there was anything to gain by moving or by eating or by anything at all.

He got up anyway. He didn't know what else to do. He had his light breakfast of fruit. He couldn't bear to go into the music room, so he sat in the lounge waiting to be hungry enough for a proper breakfast.

There used to be a piano store, he remembered. Nearby. Maybe they'd let him play for a while.

He'd never liked playing other pianos. When he was younger, when he was less than he had become, he'd had to play other pianos in performances. It was never the same; it was hollow and stilted, and although no one ever said they noticed, he felt the coldness of his own performances. As soon as he could, he had his own piano moved to wherever it was needed. Too much, some people thought, but they didn't understand. The story was better when it was told on his piano.

But this was different, this was just for him, this would be worth it.

At the thought he had a sudden burst of energy. He decided to make an omelette for breakfast instead of just frying some eggs.

By nine he was putting on his hat and coat and walking out of his front door. He walked purposely, and a little faster than usual. The day was muggy and it looked like rain. Rain didn't

65

bother him, though; if it was too heavy, he'd wait it out at the music shop.

He reached the parade of shops nearest his house. He'd thought this was where it was but there was only a record shop, not one for instruments. He wasn't worried. There were a few sets of shops like this, he'd just gone to the wrong one. He pressed on.

He passed three separate rows of shops before he really started to lose hope. His knee was aching and he was finding it increasingly difficult to breathe.

He was suddenly exhausted.

There was a girl standing on the other side of the road. She had a heavy-looking bag over one shoulder and was looking from one end of the street to the other. He crossed over to her.

'Good morning,' he said. 'I wonder, do you happen to know where the piano shop is? I'm certain there's one in the area, but I've been unable to find it.'

The girl stared, wild-eyed. She swallowed once and mutely shook her head.

'Oh. All right, then. Do you know if there are any other shops in walking distance of here? I was sure, you see, that there was a piano shop somewhere around.'

The girl's wide eyes suddenly filled with tears. 'No,' she whispered, as if it was the most shameful confession she'd ever had to make. 'I don't.'

'Well, that's OK.'

'It's the third time.'

'What's that?'

'It's the third time I haven't known. I don't know where anything is. I don't know what's wrong with me.'

'Don't you worry about it, young lady. There's no reason for you to know exactly where I want to go.'

'But I should know. I've always known. It doesn't make any sense.'

'Is there anything I can help you with at all?' he asked cautiously.

'Oh god, no, sorry. I'm being ridiculous. Sorry I can't help you.'

The girl gave each end of the street another glance, screwed up her face and headed off in a direction she appeared to have chosen at random. He looked after her in concern, and headed back the way he'd come.

He wended his way past the disappointing shops and walked up his street. He opened his door and stepped inside. He stood in the entrance of his empty and silent house. There was nothing to do now but wait for the day to pass.

Robert.

ROBERT WAS SEVERAL PER CENT sure he was going crazy. Either that, or he'd been crazy for a few years, going to a made-up job in a made-up building, and all of a sudden he'd recovered.

He was standing on the footpath in front of where his building wasn't. Where it should have been. He'd been standing there for twenty minutes. The whole ride in he'd been trying to convince himself that he'd had a strange dream about the previous day, in which he'd tried to go to work and it had disappeared and he'd wandered around London instead of sitting at a desk. It was frustrating to have wasted all that mental energy. He needn't have bothered, it was much less effort to consign it all to insanity.

It occurred to him that he could ask someone in one of the nearby buildings what had happened. He didn't want to admit to himself how much the idea of doing this terrified him, so before he could think about it too hard he marched into the hotel, loins a-girded.

The girl at the check-in counter was lovely, all honey-coloured tresses and winsome eyes. Robert wanted above all things for her not to think he was a madman. He strode to the desk trying to appear purposeful and direct.

'Hello,' he began, setting his jaw and in general doing his best to create the impression that the question he was about to ask was not a stupid one. 'I was just wondering if you knew what happened to the building next door?'

The girl raised an eyebrow and blinked in surprise. 'Next door to where?' she asked.

'Next door to here. On the left.'

'Why? What happened there?'

'I don't know. I was hoping you could tell me.'

The girl looked around for back up, but she was on her own.

'There was a building there, you see,' continued Robert. 'A white stone building with a cheap-looking statue of Artemis in the lobby that actually cost a horrendous amount of money. I was wondering if you knew what had happened to it.'

'Oh, I'm sorry, sir, I've only worked here for three months. I guess I could ask someone else for you?' The girl's hand hovered over the phone on her desk as she looked at him enquiringly.

'No, that's fine, it's been within that time. You would have seen it.'

'Really? I don't remember it. When were you last there?'

'Tuesday.'

'Tuesday?'

'Yes.'

'Tuesday this week?'

'Two days ago, yes.'

'Oh.'

Robert stared at the girl, whose eyes were wide and bewildered. He felt as if he was going to start crying. Or like he was going to faint. Or maybe run out into the street, rip his shirt off and scream into the sky.

Instead he quietly said 'thank you' and left.

In a daze, he walked back down the street towards the station. In a daze, he passed through the ticket barrier. The train was delayed for thirty-five minutes at Kings Cross and he didn't notice. He stood outside his front door for three minutes and forty-one seconds before opening it. He had no idea what he would say when he went inside. He had no idea what he was supposed to do now.

Cassie.

'Hey,' said a voice close to Cassie's head.

She was standing with her eyes closed, trying to ignore the stares. Trying to be somewhere else.

There was a security guard standing in front of her when she opened her eyes, one of the younger ones.

'Hey,' he said again. 'Hi.'

Cassie looked at him and didn't reply.

'I was just wondering if you wanted me to find those screens again,' the security guard, Jasper, according to his name tag, went on.

'What?' said Cassie.

'The other day you had screens. To give you a bit of privacy. Do you want me to get them back for you?'

'Oh,' said Cassie. 'I don't know. No, I think. They make me feel like I'm in a hospital or something. I didn't like them.'

'Fair enough. I'm Jasper, by the way. You give me a shout if you need anything.'

'I'm fine.'

'You just give me a shout.'

Jasper walked off slowly, leaving Cassie alone, or as alone as she could be. There were still debarking passengers to stare at her, and flight attendants to walk past her a little too close, saying 'My god, she's still here.'

There was still her mother, dozing quietly a few metres away. There were lots of people. There was no Floss. There was no Floss, there was no Cassie.

Delia.

DELIA WALKED QUICKLY THROUGH THE park until she found
an empty bench. With a gasp of relief, she collapsed onto it,
reminding herself to just sit, and not to curl up into the foetal
position. She closed her eyes and let the sun shine onto her face
and it was all she could do not to moan aloud in a mix of pleasure
and panic.

She stayed there for longer than she could tell, letting her fear
be stilled by her inactivity. She'd told her mother she'd be out for
two hours at most. She'd taken the tube and got out two blocks
from the square she was aiming for. It had taken her an hour and
a half to find it.

She stayed still.

When she opened her eyes she found she was no longer alone
on the bench. A man was sitting at the other end and he was
looking at her. She felt a rising tide of embarrassment and reached
for her bag to go, but before she stood the man spoke.

'How do you do that?'

'What?'

'Sorry. I was staring. Rude. You just looked so relaxed. I don't
think I know how to do that.'

'How to look relaxed? It's easy. You don't even have to actually
be relaxed, as it turns out.'

'You mean, you're not?'

'Oh, Christ.' Delia laughed. 'Not at all. I'm terrified.'

'Of what?'

'That I won't be able to find my way home, mainly.'

'Oh, well. It's a scary city if you haven't lived here for that long.'

'I've lived here my entire life. I've lived in the same house since I was born. I just wandered around this area for almost two hours trying to get here, to get to a park I've known for as long as I can remember, and I'm terrified beyond belief that when I try to leave I'll become irrevocably lost. That I'll never find my way home again. That I'll die, broken and alone, with no idea where I even am.'

'Today?'

'Well, eventually, you know.'

'Oh.'

'Sorry. I'm not crazy.' She paused. 'Oh god, I am. I am crazy. That's the only explanation for what's happened.'

'What's happened?'

'I, well, I've just lost my sense of direction. Completely.'

'Oh.'

'You don't think it's that big a thing. But that's just because you've no idea. Yesterday I left my house. I walked around the corner, around one corner, and I couldn't find my way back. To my own house. How can that happen? I stood there for about half an hour trying to figure it out and then this old man came up looking for help and he was so sad and polite and I just freaked out at him completely and ran away. The wrong way, as it turned out. Was gone for hours, my mother was terrified, it was a disaster.'

'You live with your mother?'

'Yeah, well. I'm her carer, I suppose.'

'Why does your mother need a carer?'

'She was in an accident.' Delia said. She paused for a moment before adding, 'Sometimes I suspect she doesn't need one, really. But she thinks she does, and the compensation allowed for one, so.'

'What happened?'

'She was hit by a van. She was hit by a Fortnum and Mason's van.'

'Wow.'

'I know.'

'So you both live off that?'

'We have done for five years. It was a lot. It was a lot of money. Although, it's amazing how much she can spend now she doesn't have to worry about it. I don't think she has any idea how much she goes through so quickly. Mind you, if she did know, it would mean nothing, it would bear no relation to how much we have to live on. It's weird, really, because until the accident she must have been very aware of that kind of thing. She raised me alone, so of course she was. Then the accident and she's all, 'Oh, OK, your job now,' and simultaneously stops caring about or under-standing life's minutiae. Oh god, this is boring. Why haven't you stopped me going on?'

'I've been asking you.'

'Oh right. Sorry.'

'Don't be. I'm Anthony, by the way.'

'I'm Delia. It's nice to meet you. You're not English.'

'I am actually. I haven't lived here since I was eighteen, though, so it's not surprising I don't quite have the accent. I went to New Zealand for a year, and then just stayed. I moved back with my son about six months ago.'

'With your son? Just the two of you?'

'Yeah. Just me and Jake.'

Delia bit her lip and looked down. She didn't say anything.

'Look, I have to go,' said Anthony. 'Do you come here a lot?'

'Not really,' said Delia. 'And if I wanted to, there's no guarantee I'd find my way back again.'

'Oh. Well, it was nice to meet you.'

Delia didn't watch him as he left. She stayed sitting on her bench for a couple of minutes then, suddenly restless, picked up her bag and headed towards the water.

After taking almost three hours to get home, she wasn't surprised to find her mother a little frantic.

'We've no tea,' she said as Delia entered. 'I need a cup of tea and I thought you said you'd put it somewhere reachable, but the box was empty.'

'There's a shop on the corner, Mum. Did you not think of popping down to get some?'

There was a dark pause.

'You know I can't do that. Why would you say something like that?'

'It's not that far. There are no steps on the way.'

'Well, anyway, you can go now, can't you?'

'I . . .' started Delia. 'It's just, it might take me a while.'

'Why? It's just on the corner, you said so yourself.'

'Fine. Fine. See you soon.'

Back outside the front door, Delia concentrated, trying to pin down the route to the shop in her mind. She stepped out to the footpath, and turned right. And wrong.

Mrs Featherby.

THERE IS NO PREPARING A person for having someone call their attention by shouting and rattling the thick plastic that stands in place of an erstwhile front wall. Mrs Featherby sighed as she remembered the elegant chime of the doorbell that had been in the middle of the door that had been in the middle of the wall, or the quiet rat-a-tat of the knocker beneath it. She thought wistfully of how rarely she'd heard either of them used, and sighed again.

Since the disappearance of her wall, the plastic had been pounded at least four times every day. While Mrs Featherby was willing to concede that one or two of the interferences were kindly meant, most were simply scandalised curiosity, ineffectively hidden. Certainly, the two teenage girls with the uncomfortably tight trousers had been much more agog than was generally acceptable for a social call. Then there was the middle-aged man who had seemed immune to Mrs Featherby's strongest hints that he should leave. Mrs Featherby had had to use all her skills of deception and evasion, which had been superfluous for years. Later, she reflected that it had actually been rather nice to try them out again, despite the inconvenience of having to.

The years she'd spent crafting a reputation for being reclusive seemed entirely wasted. One simply cannot be a believable recluse when one is cursed with a transparent wall.

The pungent man who claimed to be from next door had been talking about his trouble with his third cat for nearly a quarter of an hour and Mrs Featherby was struggling to find a polite reason to make him leave. She had never had a pet of any kind, so she was having difficulty empathising with Queen Victoria's constant need to vomit.

Mrs Featherby had never been able to see the benefit of having a creature in the house that was constantly making demands on you while giving you no reward. You had to do everything: feed, clean, and even, so Mrs Featherby understood, brush teeth. And if they became ill or died you were expected to have an emotional response. It all sounded like an exhausting and ultimately meaningless investment.

The man kept talking, undeterred by how indistinct and noncommittal Mrs Featherby's responses were. For some reason he used the cat's name all the time. He never once referred to her as 'she'. Slowly, as he was repeating the phrase 'Queen Victoria', Mrs Featherby became aware of a familiar but long-forgotten feeling trickling through her.

She didn't think the cat's name was Queen Victoria. In fact, she wondered if her pungent neighbour even had a third cat.

Mrs Featherby was distracted by this thought, distracted enough to stop looking for a way to extricate herself from the conversation without breaching the dictates of etiquette. Distracted enough to not notice the pungent man was grinding to a halt.

However, it did not lessen her relief to have him gone. He'd been the fourth unwanted visitor that day and irritation was high.

The temptation was, of course, to remain as far from the front of her house and the attendant inquisition as possible, but that would be deeply unsatisfying. To allow such a mischance to rule her behaviour, Mrs Featherby had decided, would be allowing circumstance to have more control than choice. She had always taken her afternoon tea in the sitting room. She had always read in the wing chair by the fireplace and always done her sewing by the window. What was the use of a sitting room in which she could not sit?

This was the question she put to the builder the third time she called him to check on his progress.

'Right,' Bruno said. 'Yep, I understand that. Naturally. But if you'll remember, Mrs F, I did suggest that you might like to find somewhere else to stay.'

'That would be a far more inconvenient thing for me to do, I'm afraid. All I wish to ascertain is how much longer I am going to have to exist in this state of constant interruption.'

'You want to know when I'll be able to fix your wall?'

'I wish to know when you'll be able to fix my wall.'

'Well, the good news is, I've found a place I can source matching bricks.'

'That is excellent news.'

'Yes, well. It is actually, they weren't that easy to track down.'

'Believe me, you have my full respect for having done so.'

'Sure. Cheers for that. Thing is, though, they're not that common, those bricks, anymore. There's not a high demand, see, so the supplier I've managed to find, doesn't carry large numbers of them as a matter of course. So he can get them in for me, not a problem there, per say, but he's not sure how long he'll have to wait. And obviously, I have to wait until he has them. And—'

'And I, in turn, must wait until they are with you.'

'Yeah.'

Mrs Featherby sighed again, quietly.

'What's the biggest hassle, there, Mrs F? Is it getting too cold? Or is the plastic too noisy? I can throw up another layer, try and insulate it better. See if there's a way I can weight it down so it doesn't move as much, that kind of thing.'

'Oh, well, if you could, I'm sure that would be lovely. There's not much you can do to stop the people, I'm afraid.'

'The people?'

'Yes. They will insist on trying to talk to me. Asking all kinds of impertinent questions about what's going on. They seem to have forgotten that a person in their house is still in private domicile, even If the walls are made of plastic.'

'Is it so bad? Talking to people?'

'What do you mean?'

'Conversation, love. Doesn't kill you.'

'You will let me know, won't you? When you'll be able to start work?'

'Oh, course, course. Soon as poss, Mrs F.'

Mrs Featherby stood for a moment after the phone call. She didn't want to go back through to the front of the house, but there was knitting to be done, and there was only one place she was happy to do it.

Robert.

ROBERT STOOD JUST INSIDE THE front door listening to Mara and Bonny in the kitchen. They were reading a story but stopping to giggle too much for him to be able to tell what it was. After a few minutes he realised he'd left the door open behind him. At the sound of it closing, Mara came through.

'Hello,' she said. 'What are you doing home? Is everything OK?'

'Um, I kind of lost my job.'

'What do you mean? You were fired? What for?'

'No. No, I don't think so. I mean it would be a pretty elaborate way of firing someone. And it would cost, just, untold millions. And a lot of people. And time. The logistics of the thing would be staggering and I'm pretty sure it'd be hard to get council permission. And to get it done in the time it took, well, that would be absurd. Unless there's more going on than we're aware of. Like maybe they can actually freeze time or something.'

'They?' said Mara. 'What are you talking about?'

Robert took a deep breath and tried to look his sanest. 'I can't find my job. I've just lost it.'

'You've lost it.'

'Yep. I can't find it.'

'Rob, I am 100 per cent confused right now.'

'Oh god, me too.'

'What's going on?'

'OK, so, yesterday I went to work, at least I tried to, but it wasn't there. So I freaked out, you know, and spent the whole day just wandering around until it occurred to me to come home. And then there was the whole debacle about Bonny and by the end of that I just thought that maybe I'd made it up, you know, had a weird daydream on the tube. But then this morning, the same thing. I went to work, the same place I've been going for the last several years, and nothing.'

'You mean, what, the building's fallen down?'

'No. I mean it's not there. There's no gap, there's nothing new in its place, it's just not there.'

'OK. You understand that there's no way this can have actually happened, right?'

'Oh, I know. This is very against the laws of physics.'

'Bloody hell. Bloody hell. I just . . . I don't . . . Can you show me?'

Forty minutes later the three of them were stood on the street where Robert used to work.

'Bloody hell,' said Mara. 'How . . .? What . . .? Let's go for ice cream.'

'You're the best girl in the world.'

'I am aware of it.' Mara shot Robert an appraising look before turning and walking down the street with Bonny. He looked back at where his building should be one more time before following after them.

Cassie.

ALMOST TWO WEEKS AFTER CASSIE'S roots appeared, her mother called in an arborist. She'd tried a podiatrist first, who said that as far as he could see, the complaint wasn't specifically related to Cassie's feet, although it had started there. He told them he could rule out verrucae and suggested they ask someone else. The next person to examine Cassie was a gynaecologist, which Cassie didn't understand. As far as she could tell, the fact that she was turning into a tree was nothing to do with the fact that she was female, but her mother insisted they try. The last medical professional was a surgeon, whose opinion was that the safest bet would be to amputate Cassie's feet just below the knee, although she did admit that she couldn't guarantee that the bark wouldn't simply reappear over the stumps. Cassie had thought her mother might punch her.

All any of the doctors were willing to categorically state was that Cassie's feet had become distinctly plant-based. And were continuing to do so, for the bark was spreading. After one day it had reached halfway up her feet, to the spot where two or three long blonde hairs were wont to grow. After two days it was cresting around the pairs of bumps on either side of her ankles. Cassie had watched it for hours, certain that at this rate of growth she should be able to detect movement, but she never could. After two weeks it was approaching her knees.

The arborist was a squat woman in her fifties. She wore a strange hodgepodge of clothes that seemed specifically designed to not match. Her long, flyaway hair was piled up on her head and topped with a knitted hat that a five-year-old child might have worn in stripes of purple and orange. She wore a shirt, a couple of sizes too big, which had once been smart and had a pinstripe running through it, but that had evidently been much worn. It was clear that a lot of the wearing had been done in a garden or forest or glade. Over that was a military jacket with several medals pinned to the lapel. Her feet were besandalled and her trousers were flared.

She said nothing as she approached Cassie, simply looked her up and down once before focusing on her feet. She knelt down and looked closely at the bark. She tugged gently at one of the roots. She leaned forward and gave a long sniff, breathing in the aroma.

Cassie's mother gasped as the arborist pulled out a small, gleaming knife. She swiftly and deftly flicked the knife over Cassie's left foot, down and up again in one fluid motion. Cassie gave a sharp intake of breath and her mother cried out.

'Did you feel that?' asked the arborist, looking Cassie in the eye for the first time.

'Yes,' said Cassie. 'Not on my foot, really. Just, I just felt it. In general.'

'Hmm,' said the arborist. She'd removed her gaze from Cassie's face and was looking at the sliver of wood she'd just carved out of Cassie. It was very thin but wide. The arborist had sliced deep into Cassie's foot. She looked closely at the sliver for some time.

'Well,' she said, finally, getting to her feet. 'It looks like willow.'

'She's turning into a willow tree?' asked Cassie's mother.

'Looks that way. Worrying. Willows like a lot of moisture. Not really suited to airport terminals.'

'But how do we stop it?'

'Stop what?'

'Stop it happening. How do we stop her turning into a tree?'

The arborist looked from Cassie to her mother and back again. 'In these cases of spontaneous transformation—'

'So it's happened before?'

The arborist blinked at the interruption. 'What?'

'You've seen this before?'

'No. No, not at all, not at all, not me. Not anyone I know. But there are stories, you know. There have always been stories.'

'What stories?'

'Well. Girls that turn into trees for protection or for money or what have you.'

'How do they turn back?'

'Turn back? Well. Sometimes they do, that is true. But those are the parts of the stories that always seem the least plausible. Using the right kind of jug to water the tree, or even pronouncing some kind of spell. Ha! As if words are going to have any effect on a tree. Idiocy. Anyway, even if you allow for that kind of nonsense, it hardly ever goes well, hardly ever. Branches have come off, you know, so the girls will be missing arms and such like. But the girls that stay as they are, well. Sometimes it's been the creation of a whole new kind of tree, and who wouldn't want that?'

'Who wouldn't – what?'

'It's all right, Mum,' said Cassie. Her voice felt rougher and deeper than it had been. 'I have to stay here anyway. Floss is coming here. I don't need to move.'

'Yes, you do, love. You need to come home. You need to sleep in your bed and eat some good food. And you need to start thinking about the possibility that Floss isn't coming.'

'She is.'

'Seems to me she'd have been here by now. Seems to me she'd have called you.'

'I'm staying here. It doesn't matter what my feet look like. Floss doesn't care what my feet look like.'

Cassie's mum turned back to the arborist. 'How can we stop it happening?'

'Oh, you can't. It'll be interesting to see it progress, though.'

'So there's nothing we can do? We just lose hope?'

'Lose hope in what? Nature? Quite the reverse, it's a sign that we should never lose hope in nature. This is a fascinating occurrence.'

'I am losing my daughter! This isn't fascinating, this is horrific. Are you saying there's no chance that this, whatever it is, is going to reverse itself?'

'That's what's so exciting! I have no idea. I've never seen this before. As far as I know no one's ever seen it before, at least not recently enough for it to be anything but legend now. We don't know what started it happening, we don't know what'll keep it going or what could stop it. There's just so much to discover.'

Cassie could sense an impending rise in her mother's pitch and she wondered if she could prevent it.

'Mum,' she said. 'Mum.' She waited a moment for the sound of her voice to register. Her mother coughed a little in the attempt to cease hysterics.

'Mum,' said Cassie again. 'It's OK. It's not like I want to leave here anyway. I have to stay.'

'Cassie, I know you want to stay, but you shouldn't. You should be coming home and living your life. And even if you are staying it should be because you're a grumpy, stubborn, wilful girl, not because you're physically unable to move. Not because you're turning into a bloody tree. It's just not right.'

'It's just my feet, Mum. Never liked them anyway. I'm fine. It's fine.'

Jake.

Jake's jersey is covered in tiny droplets of water as he stands on the
footpath facing his house. It looks like a ghostly imitation of itself.
It is raining, but not properly raining. It is the sort of rain that
feels like it's hovering, rather than falling. It's almost mist, except
without the mystery. Fine drops of water float morosely through
the air, finding clothes and eyelashes to cling to.
Jake wishes he'd gone back inside with his mother. She'd gone
to get a recipe for the smiling lady. The smiling lady is friends
with Mel, who is friends with Jake's mum, but the smiling lady
is not friends with Jake's mum. Jake's mum doesn't really like
her and is annoyed about having promised her the recipe.
She said she'd be quick but it's been ages and she's not back yet
and Jake's hair is now uncomfortably damp.
Jake wishes he didn't have to go to the doctor. It didn't seem to
him like there was anything particularly the matter with his
knees and feet anyway. He didn't know why people kept picking
on them. If he didn't have to go to the doctor he could be
inside playing or reading. Except if he didn't have to go the
doctor he'd have to be at school. Jake sighed.
He stumbled when the ground moved, but only a little. He
didn't fall. The house fell, but Jake stayed standing.

Jake sighed. He couldn't remember, he couldn't know for certain.
Surely, when he figured out the right weather he would be able

86

to tell. He would know what that day had been like. It would make sense.

Jake was eating breakfast alone. No, his dad was there. He and his dad were eating breakfast at the same time. He suddenly felt like his dad had been talking to him, had been asking him questions, and he hadn't even noticed.

'What?' he said.

'Do you want to go out for burgers tonight?' his dad said. 'We haven't done a boys' night out for ages.'

'Oh. Sure.'

They sat with their toast, silently, companionably. Chewing. When they were finished, Jake's dad took both of the plates to the sink and washed them. He looked at Jake, nodded a couple of times, and went down the hall to his office.

Jake wasn't really sure if he did want to go out for burgers. He wasn't sure he wanted to spend a whole evening talking to his dad. He had other things on his mind.

Marcus.

HE NOTICED HE WASN'T WEARING shoes when he was in the middle of the shop. He didn't know what to do. Pointless to go home, really, wasn't it, just to put on shoes and come all the way back. All he wanted to do was buy milk. A man could buy milk, if he wanted, without shoes. And salt, he needed salt.

He looked around. There were only a few people. They wouldn't mind, there was no reason to think they'd mind. They probably had their own concerns, probably didn't care at all about an old man's naked feet.

He was standing by the pet food. That wasn't right. He didn't have any pets. Had never wanted any. People had suggested he get a cat after Albert died, but he hadn't. Hadn't seen the point.

How had he got all the way to the shop without noticing he wasn't wearing shoes or socks? How had he not felt the concrete on the soles of his feet? He hoped he hadn't stepped in something, or on something, without noticing it.

A hand landed on his shoulder and he turned around.

'Dad?' she looked upset. 'What's going on?'

'I needed some milk,' he said. 'I had to come and buy some milk. And some salt. I need milk and salt.'

'You said you'd be home for the piano man. He called me because no one was home. I've been waiting for you for almost half an hour.'

How long had he been standing here? How long had he been staring at pet food he didn't need?

'What did he say? The piano man, what did he say? Can he fix it?'

'Yeah, he's fixing it now.'

'He's fixing it. He's fixing it now. He's fixing my piano.'

His daughter looked at him closely.

'Are you all right?' she asked.

He couldn't answer immediately. He swallowed and let out a grunt.

He'd spent hours over that piano, with his father, when he was twenty-one. Years before Albert, years before her; when he was deciding who he was going to be. He'd restored that piano and as he'd done so, he'd built himself; it was more a part of him than anything else he had.

'Dad, I don't know what to do.'

'Salt. I need salt.'

'Dad, where are your shoes?'

She didn't speak all the way home. She was silent as she opened the front door. Strange, for her. She'd always been a chatterer. She went to the kitchen and got out the kettle, but she didn't fill it. She put it on the bench beside the sink and walked round and round. She'd never been able to hide the way she felt. She was far more expressive than he or Albert had ever been. He had always though it strange that she had made no effort to pursue the arts, having been raised as she had by him and Albert. She'd always been far more interested in science. He now thought it was because she didn't need any more expression than her face already gave her. With a face like that, had she been interested in the arts, she could have been an actress. Like her mother.

He was glad she preferred science.

He watched his girl now: her mouth constantly moving, her lips pressing together, then coming apart, her tongue moving over her teeth. Searching for something to say.

'I'm all right,' he said. 'I just need to be able to play. I just need some music.'

'I know.' She sighed. He hated making her sigh. She was not made for sighs.

Delia.

WHAT WAS HAPPENING TO DELIA had been happening for years, although she hadn't noticed it. The first symptom showed itself seven months and five days after the accident. That was the day her mother felt strong enough to get dressed by herself for the first time. It was the day she almost managed to get from her bed to her wheelchair without help, and Delia could tell she'd get there within a few days.

It was the day Delia's mother said, 'Soon you won't have to look after me so much. Soon you'll be able to start finishing your degree.'

It was the day Delia stood in front of her old bedroom door. It was the day she stood there and thought about all the boxes of notes, of all the textbooks, of the so nearly finished dissertation. It was the day she stood in front of the door and didn't open it.

Right up until the moment when she didn't open the door, Delia had been looking forward to starting her studies again. Right up until that moment she'd planned to take out her carefully filed notes and read over what she'd written so far, and decide whether she wanted to reconsider her angle. She'd thought about whether she wanted to work for a while or do further study. She'd browsed the internet for PHD options. But for some reason, when she stood in front of that door, she couldn't figure out whether or not she wanted to open it. She had no reason for not wanting to open it, she just didn't know whether she wanted to. So she didn't.

Delia's mother was not an observant or thoughtful woman. As the weeks went by, she failed to ask when Delia was planning to keep studying. As the months passed, she didn't ask whether Delia was going to do something else. As the years changed, she didn't ask what Delia wanted.

She had always believed Delia's teachers when they wrote on all those report cards that Delia was driven, that she was focused and ambitious. She'd always been proud that people could say that about her daughter, but she'd never been one to say those things herself. She'd never noticed what it was about her that made her teachers so regularly make such comments. And she didn't notice as that direction began to fade.

Neither did Delia.

They also didn't notice it when, two years later, Delia stopped deciding what they should have for dinner. She made the same three indifferent meals in sequence, week after week, month after month, without thinking. They didn't notice when she stopped thinking about what clothes she wanted to wear, or what she wanted to do with her hair, and instead started cycling through her most comfort-able clothes in the order they were hanging in her closet, and throwing her hair haphazardly into a structurally unsound pile on her head.

They didn't notice it start and they didn't notice it getting worse, until suddenly Delia couldn't find her way anywhere at all.

So it happened one day that she got lost in the middle of Trafalgar Square. She hadn't decided to go there; she just came across the tube station and got on a train. She'd got out at the other end, and found herself in front of the National Portrait Gallery. She hadn't been able to decide whether she should go inside. She hadn't been there in years.

She walked around a bit while she thought about whether or not she should visit the gallery, and two minutes later she was standing beside a lion, completely lost.

She knew where she was, obviously, but she didn't know how to get anywhere else. She didn't know how to get back to the gallery, but then she still didn't know whether she wanted to go in. She didn't know how to get to the tube station, even though she knew it was right beside the square. She didn't know how long she'd been standing there, lost beside a lion.

'Wow,' someone said. 'Hello again.'

Delia blinked. It was the man from the park.

'Oh. Hello. Anthony.'

'Are you all right?'

Delia bit her lip and thought about it. She wasn't sure what was going on and she wasn't sure how worried she should be. She'd been panicked when she got lost in the park, but this time she was simply baffled.

'I,' she said. 'Yes, I'm all right. I'm lost again, but I'm OK.'

That was the moment she discovered that Anthony's face got very still when he didn't believe someone. He persuaded her to come with him for a coffee, and pointed out the entrance to Charing Cross Station on the way past.

They sat in silence for a few minutes. Delia couldn't tell if it was an awkward silence or a comfortable one. She wondered if she should start talking just in case it was the former.

'So you've a kid,' she said, awkwardly.

'Yeah.'

Delia cleared her throat and continued. 'How's he liking London?'

'He's good, I think. He's pretty relaxed, you know, pretty philosophical. I was worried, but he's doing well. He's quite quiet, you know, he's not a big talker, but he's made some friends, he gets on with the other kids. He's good at maths. He's very good at maths. But his grammar is appalling, apparently. Standards are higher here, I think. Teachers are better educated. That seems mean. Might not even be true. Anyway, Jake's doing well. I can't believe how grown up he's becoming. He used to be this gangly knock-kneed kid who never stopped talking, and now he's all tall and serious.'

'He had knock-knees?'

'Yep. And a pudding-bowl haircut. Not anymore, though. Now he looks like a proper human.'

They sat some more.

'What did your mother do?' Anthony asked. 'Before the accident?'

'She had a bookshop.'

'She can't still do that?'

'I don't know. I guess she doesn't think so. Tall shelves, not much room, you know. And she'd have to leave the house.'

'Right. Why doesn't she want to leave the house?'

'I don't actually know.' Delia said. 'Whenever I try to encourage her to, she gets petulant and awful. So now she embroiders.'

'She embroiders?'

'She only embroiders. She doesn't do anything else. Ever. She doesn't even watch television, so we don't have one in the house.'

'Jake decided he wanted to try that once. Embroidery, I mean, not the not watching television. He asked his mum to teach him, but she was terrible at it, was never good at sewing-related activities actually, so I had to take over. Our biggest achievement was a ten-inch-square picture of a pair of gorillas that we very nearly finished.'

By this point they'd finished their coffees and Delia didn't know whether she wanted another one so she stood up.

'Will you be OK?' asked Anthony as they left. 'Do you want me to help you get home?'

'No,' said Delia, too abruptly. 'I'll be fine. I just need to make it to the tube station. Which is just over there, right?'

'Sure. I mean, it's more in the other direction. But you were close.'

'Right. If by close you mean incredibly far away.'

'I should help you get home.'

'Absolutely not. I will not be a girl who's literally lost without a man.'

'But you'd be happy to be that figuratively?'

'Thank you. I'll be fine.'

'You know the way home from the station at the other end?'

Delia knew she didn't. She knew by now the chances of her getting out of the station and knowing where to go were a pale shadow in a dimly lit room by this point, but there's a limit to how often you can admit to being lost in one day.

'Don't worry. I'll be OK.'

Anthony was silent for a moment. 'Can you just call me if you're not?' He held out a card.

Delia didn't reply.

'You're not a helpless woman who needs help from a man to do something women can't do, you know. You're a human that needs help with something she's finding difficult, just at the moment.'

'Fine.' She reached out a hand and took his card. 'I'll call you if it takes me more that two hours to find my house.'

'One hour.'

'An hour and a half.'

'One hour.'

'No deal.'

'Good lord, woman.'

'It's an hour and a half or I'm not calling at all.'

'You leave me with no choice.'

'Deal with it.' Delia grinned suddenly. It was at that moment that she learned that Anthony's left cheek crinkled more than his right when he smiled.

She thought about that crinkle a lot as she walked from the station to her house, unaware that she circled it four times before finding it.

Robert.

IT WAS THE MIDDLE OF the night and Robert lay awake as the numbers on the clock changed. In his mind he was filling out a job application. Trying to fill out a job application. It wasn't for any job in particular, he hadn't bothered to imagine that far. All the applications he'd looked at and failed to complete over the last couple of weeks had become indistinguishable from one another so there was no need to be specific in fraught late-night fantasies. All the time now there was a phantom phalanx of HR officers hovering over him as he stared at questions he no longer had any answers to. What is your previous work experience? Why did you leave your last job? Who are your referees?

How was he supposed to convince someone that his inability to account for the last six years of his working life was no reason not to give him a new job?

He tried to construct an elaborate explanation that would be more believable than the sudden vanishing of his workplace. He could say he'd spent a few years caring for an elderly aunt well off the grid in the highlands, although he'd have to try to reverse the Londoning that had happened to his accent over the years. He could say that when he got married he decided to be a home maker for a few years while Mara worked. He could claim to have spent a few years travelling, exploring the hidden and dangerous areas of deepest Africa, and only now came to realise that the world he'd left, the world he'd studied, the world of corporate finance was really where his heart lay.

The main problem with the lie option, apart from the impossibility of choosing between the available options, was that Robert had never successfully lied in his life. He was pathologically honest. It was a problem.

Part of him was relieved every time he let himself give up on a vacancy. Now that he'd stopped working, now that he was thinking about what he should be doing, everything he was qualified for seemed strangely unappealing. He wanted to find something to do, he just wasn't sure what, and the more he thought about it the less clear it became.

And there was another, less important, but somehow equally unsettling problem.

Robert was bored. It was a long time since he'd been bored. Well, he'd been bored by what he was doing sometimes, but he'd never actually had nothing to do. Not that there was nothing to do entirely; he'd been able to take charge of Bonny's continued education, which left Mara free to work, and he was enjoying that, but it still left him with hours to fill every afternoon.

It was nice for a few days. He read books he'd been lent months earlier. He weeded the garden. But it wasn't long before the guilt at being so unproductive began to rub away at him.

He couldn't rid himself of the feeling that he should be achieving more with his time. That he should be achieving anything at all. That he shouldn't be wasting his days.

Cassie.

THE CLEANERS WERE THE FIRST to notice the floor – naturally. Few people pay close attention to the floor in an airport, there are generally much more important concerns.

It happened like this:

Cherry, the cleaner Cassie liked the least, the one who stared and never spoke, was polishing the floor on the far side of the terminal.

Cassie didn't know, because she'd never tried to find out, but Cherry had been cleaning the airport terminals for twenty years to support her daughter, who was deaf. Cherry herself was deeply superstitious and believed the deafness was due to a curse.

Cherry was using the floor buffer over by the least popular of the cafes when it suddenly shuddered and stopped. She slapped the side of it and pressed its big red button and it shuddered some more. After a few more tries and three solid kicks, she picked up her radio. Cassie watched her from across the hall as she spoke into the handset, her free left arm flailing wildly in the air. She watched as Cherry returned the radio to the holster and waited.

It was Burt who came to Cherry's aid. Burt had a daughter, and his daughter had too many boyfriends. He smiled at Cassie when he saw her, but in a manner that was clearly based on trying to avoid conversation.

Burt approached Cherry and Cherry threw her hands in the air, wailing about how the machine hated her, how it had been battling her from the first, how it was out to get her, how she wouldn't let it see her cry.

Burt pressed the big red button. He kicked the machine. He pressed the button again. He sighed.

Eventually the two of them got the machine onto its side and, on their hands and knees, started peering at its undercarriage. Cherry put her hand deep into the bowels of the beast and pulled out something that appeared to be blocking it.

She and Burt stared at the green mulch in her hand.

They looked up at one another's confused faces.

They looked at the floor.

Slowly, Burt put out his hand and ran it over the surface of the floor. He grasped something between his thumb and forefinger and pulled at it. He held it up in front of Cherry's eyes, which were rounded in amazement.

Sticking out from between Burt's fingers was a slender and perky blade of grass.

The two cleaners gazed down at the sparse lawn spreading over the floor beneath them. From their unusually low angle, it was so apparent they wondered how they'd missed it up until this point. The grass seemed to get thicker further away from them, the green hue it gave the floor getting stronger as it neared the bark-covered feet of Cassie, until it faded into the white corners in the distance.

Burt pulled out his own radio and spoke into it. Cassie watched from the other side of the room as Burt and Cherry stood and waited.

Eventually they were joined by the security guard. The young security guard. Jasper.

Cherry hung back with her arms crossed as Burt talked to Jasper. He pointed at the floor and at Cassie and at the floor again. Jasper ran a hand over his face, nodded a couple of times and ambled over to Cassie.

'Hey,' he said. 'What's up?'

'Hi,' said Cassie.

'Right,' said Jasper. 'The thing is, we've had a complaint.' He cracked a knuckle nervously.

'About me?'

'Not really. Kind of. You looked at the floor recently?'

Cassie was confused. She didn't like looking at the floor. No one does, really, it's always so much dirtier than we like to think, but for Cassie it was also the place where she didn't have any feet.

'No,' she said. 'Do you . . . Do you want me to?'

'Oh, yes please,' said Jasper.

Cassie stared at him for a moment before glancing down.

'Oh,' she said. 'It's green. The floor's green. What have you done to it?'

'I haven't done anything. No one's done anything. It's grass. There's grass growing on the floor. Of the airport.'

Cassie looked down again, her puzzled gaze travelling slowly out from where her own roots entered the floor to the further, whiter edges of the arrivals lounge.

'Oh,' she said.

'Right,' said Jasper. 'Thing is, the cleaners need to polish the floor. But they can't because of the grass. They asked me to just see if there's any way you can stop it.'

'It's not me. It's the floor that's doing it.'

'Right. There's just some debate amongst the cleaning staff about whether you're responsible for the whole, ah, situation, or, well, not. If you can do anything about it.'

'It's not my fault.'

'Right. Well. I just said I'd check.'

'You don't believe me. How am I supposed to make it stop? What do you expect me to do? I didn't start it; it's happening to me. I can't control it. I can't fight it.'

'Can you not, then?' said Jasper. 'Righto.'

Cassie watched him has he strolled back to the two cleaners. He talked to them for a moment. They didn't look happy, but they packed up their equipment and left. Jasper watched them leave and then walked back over to Cassie.

'I've told them they'll have to make other arrangements. But if you think of anything . . .'

Cassie said nothing.

Jasper looked at Cassie for a moment. He seemed undecided about something.

He signed. 'And if you need anything,' he said, as he turned to walk away, 'give me a shout.'

The Watch.

ITEM: WATCH

Place found: supermarket floor, confectionery aisle.

The tall man had had the watch all his life. It had belonged to his grandfather and didn't work, but he wore it all the time. Most of the time. When he went running he left it in the bathroom and one day, when he was travelling on business, he forgot to put it back on.

The hotel found it and called his office who confirmed that it was his. Someone in the hotel's administration department was charged with posting it back to him, but she was new and distracted and chose the envelope poorly.

By the time the envelope reached the tall man it contained only a hole in the bottom left corner.

The tall man didn't want to tell his mother that he'd lost the watch. She hadn't wanted him to have it, but his grandfather had given it to him directly just before he died. So he didn't go home for Christmas that year. Or the year after.

Delia.

Aimless wandering can be strange and romantic if you do it occasionally, unexpectedly, and in a nice place; meandering through strange towns and foreign cities, strolling down country lanes. But aimless wandering in your own neighbourhood in North London is rarely romantic or interesting, and never so when you do it on a daily basis. Your head isn't paying attention, so your feet simply follow the path you've led them down before. Your mind stops noticing, but your eyes look at the same houses and shops they've seen every day for most of forever.

Ever since the accident, Delia had been walking with no goal but that of temporary escape. She'd walked with no interest in what was around her, because there was nothing around her she hadn't expected to see. She would walk, she would turn, she would walk back, and she would notice nothing.

Now that she was lost, as soon as she walked a few metres from her front door, she'd begun to pay attention to everything around her, in a vain attempt to find her way. She was discovering streets she'd never been down, finding shops, squares, cafés.

As terrifying as it was to be completely lost, there was something about it she enjoyed, something that made it worth the fear.

On this particular day, although she didn't know it, she was walking towards the scariest place she had been in years.

She'd left the house two hours earlier, having first set her mother up with enough easily reachable food to last a village for a week.

She was walking down a street that seemed purely residential when she saw the sign. The building it was sitting outside was your common or garden brick house. It advertised weekly art classes, with one starting that evening. She found herself rooted to the spot, wide-eyed and much sweatier than she'd been a moment earlier.

She stood staring at the sign, not noticing the small, wispy man who was standing in the doorway of the house beyond.

'Yes?' he said eventually. 'Hello?'

Delia jumped. 'Oh,' she said. 'Hello. I just . . . the sign. I saw it.'

'What? Oh. Art. All right. It's, er, my wife. She's just . . . come in. I'll make you some tea.'

Delia followed the creature into a bright hallway and through to a kitchen, wiping her palms on her dress.

'She's just on the phone. Bit of a panic, I'm afraid. Sure it'll work itself out. I was just about to get some tea ready, though. Just in case. You're an artist, are you? Can't draw at all myself, I'm afraid. History. That's where I'm at home. History makes sense to me, you see. You can understand people, whole cultures, from looking at what happened to them. At what they've done. Art is, well, it's more, I suppose . . . isn't it? My wife's incredible, though, truly astounding, truly. That's hers, you know.'

He pointed to a small painting on the wall. Blocks of colour showing hills and a horizon, with a figure silhouetted against it. Somehow it looked both lonesome and hopeful.

'It's lovely.'

'Isn't it, though? Marvellous, she is.'

He spooned tea into a pot and filled it from the kettle. As it brewed he filled a plate with scones and got jam and butter out of a cupboard.

'Look good, don't they?' he said, nodding at Delia. 'Made them. Made them myself. Just out of the oven half an hour before you knocked at the door. Best thing about being retired, that. Baking.

My wife's a disaster at baking, a complete disaster. Doesn't pay attention, you see. You've got to pay attention. It's a science, getting it right.'

Just as he was bringing the tea things over to the table, a tall, gangly woman came soaring into the small kitchen.

'Well! It's all an absolute fucking catastrophe, beloved, naturally, isn't it? They've no fucking commitment, these youths of today, have they? Not to employers, not to fucking art. She may say she's ill, but I know perfectly well that she just feels fucking fat today. And try as I might to tell her that nobody fucking cares, that fat is fucking interesting, I cannot make any headway. She just gets all fucking offended, as if it's my fault she has such low fucking self-regard. Oh, hello, who are you?'

The woman peered at Delia while pulling out a battered silver cigarette case and lighting a cigarette.

'This is – oh.' The elfin little man suddenly seemed to realise he'd forgotten the niceties of introduction. 'She wants to talk about the art classes.'

'I'm Delia,' said Delia. 'The sign is what I saw. Outside.' She blinked a couple of times. She didn't know why she was suddenly so nervous.

'There may not fucking be any classes, my darling. It's all going fucking up in fucking smoke. These scones, beloved, are a marvel.'

'Thank you, my dear. Is there no one else?'

'No there bloody isn't. I've called everyone except that nymphet, Rena, Lena, whatever it was, and I'm not fucking calling her; she posed as if it were a playboy shoot or some fucking such nonsense, she was a complete fucking waste of time.'

Delia was completely overwhelmed by the magnificent person in front of her. She'd never heard such spectacular swearing.

The woman suddenly interrupted herself. 'Would you like more tea, my dear?'

'Oh, thanks, that would be lovely. What's gone wrong, exactly?'

'My fucking model's cancelled for tonight's class.'

'Is it a life drawing class?'

'Yes, yes, but there's no fucking life to draw, so I'm afraid I don't know what to tell you.'

Delia was silent for a moment. An art class had seemed exciting when she first came into the house, when she saw the painting on the wall. But when she thought about actually being in one, about having a paintbrush in her hand and a blank sheet of paper in front of her, she didn't think she could do it. She hadn't so much as doodled a flower in years.

But maybe she could be a part of the class without attending it.

'I could sit for it,' she said suddenly.

The woman stared.

'Would you actually? I thought you wanted to take the class yourself?'

'Oh,' said Delia. 'No. No, I don't want to take a class. I don't want to take an art class. No.'

'Oh. I thought that was the reason you came in. Was it not? But yes, would you fucking actually? Have you done it before? I don't want to force you into it, you know, it's not for everybody, but you would really be saving the whole thing and probably single-handedly restoring my faith in all of fucking humanity.'

'I think it would be fine.'

'Amazing. Fucking amazing. You said your name; what was your name?'

'Delia.'

'Delia, fabulous. I'm Mattie. This is Donald.'

'Charmed,' said Donald. Delia grinned.

Mrs Featherby.

THERE WAS A CHILD-SHAPED BLUR on the other side of the plastic sheet. Mrs Featherby noticed it at twenty-seven minutes past three. Certain it would disappear before long, she elected to ignore it.

At thirteen minutes to four, when it had not moved, she retreated to the kitchen, deciding it was high time she made a start on that cake she'd been meaning to bake. The two fruit loaves she'd had in the pantry had had to be thrown out that morning. She measured out flour and sugar and cracked eggs and softened butter. She whisked and stirred and mixed and when the cake was safely in the oven she thoroughly cleaned all utensils, bowls and surfaces.

There was half an hour still left on the timer and the kitchen was not a comfortable place for one to sit with one's book, so Mrs Featherby returned to the sitting room. The blur had not moved on.

Mrs Featherby stood, unsure of what to do for several moments. She edged slowly towards the blur. And more slowly, a little closer.

A gleeful voice rang out.

'I can see you!'

'Right,' said Mrs Featherby, startled. 'How splendid of you.'

'Can you see me?'

'I can, in actual fact.'

There followed a sequence of uncontrolled chortling from behind the curtain.

'This is a funny house. It didn't used to be funny, but it's funny now.'

'Yes, well. I suppose it is.'

'Does it make you laugh all of the time to live in it?'

'I can't say that it does.'

'Why?'

'Well, I suppose it's not as funny to me as it is to you.'

'OK.'

There was another voice from outside. A grown-up voice. A manly voice.

'Bonny,' it said. 'What are you doing?'

'I'm talking to the lady in the funny house. She doesn't laugh.'

'Right. Good. I'm sorry, Mrs, um.'

'Mrs Featherby,' said Mrs Featherby.

'Mrs Featherby. I'm Rob. I'm also sorry. I'll drag this rascalish she-devil away.'

'Thank you. That's quite all right.'

'Dad,' said the small girl. 'What's rascalish?'

'Someone who runs off and pesters the neighbours and makes her mother worry. Shall I teach you to spell it?'

'Not right now. Can I play a game? Can you play a game with me?'

'We can play the game of learning, young wench.'

'Oh. OK. Goodbye lady!'

Mrs Featherby stood for a few minutes before heading back through to the kitchen. She put on the kettle and waited for it to boil. She set up a tray with a teapot, one cup, and one plate with one biscuit. She spooned tea leaves into the teapot and poured in the boiled water. She carried the tray through to the sitting room and sat down.

She drank her tea and ate her biscuit and carried the tray back to the kitchen to clean up, just as the cake was ready. She iced it and slid it into the pantry, so that it would be on hand in the event of visitors, as her mother had always taught her.

Jake.

'WHY ON EARTH ARE YOU not at school, youngster? Do you ever go?'

The Voice had been in a back room when Jake entered the shop, but had come through at the sound of the door.

'I already went to school today. I was there this morning.'

'Right. Didn't realise it had become the sort of deal where you just check in once a day and you're done. You know, you used to have to stay there for upwards of several hours.'

Jake didn't answer. He was browsing the shelves.

'Do you have anything else interesting?'

'Everything's interesting.'

'Anything like before. Anything lost.'

'What do you mean?'

'I bought the book last time. The woman who sold it to you, it wasn't hers. She'd just found it somewhere. Do you have anything else like that?'

The Voice stared at him. 'You want things that didn't belong to the people that brought them in here?'

Jake beamed. 'Exactly. Yes please.'

'OK.' The Voice came further out into the shop and started looking at the shelves. 'There's a necklace somewhere that a guy found in his mother's things after she died. He'd never seen it before, and it was hidden away. Not kept with the rest of her jewellery.'

'No,' said Jake decisively. 'Not that.'

'All right. Ooh, there's this hat.' She pulled down a blue felt hat, the kind of hat that Jake had seen gangsters wearing in old movies, although he'd never seen a gangster wearing a blue one. 'A guy had just become a cabbie and he found this under the seat of the cab he bought. The cab hadn't been used in years.'

'Perfect.'

Jake paid, jammed the hat on his head, and left the shop.

He dawdled on his walk home. His head was hot. It was not hat weather.

Marcus.

He was sitting at the piano. It was seven in the morning and he'd been sitting there for forty minutes. His right hand was raised, his fingers resting gently on the keys.

He raised his left hand.

Closing his eyes he began to play a Rachmaninoff concerto. He persisted for a few bars before pulling his hands sharply away from the instrument as if they were burning.

It wasn't the same.

It was still broken.

It was not his piano.

The day the keys had been replaced he'd felt his imminent renewal building deep within himself, preparing to flow out as soon as he was able to play. He thought he'd play as soon as he was alone, but instead he waited, keeping the euphoria suppressed for the thrill of it.

Finally, this morning, he'd sat down. He'd breathed in and prepared himself. He'd begun to play. And it was useless.

He knew after half a bar that it was no good. The latent restoration of his spirits died as he removed his hands and the music faded away.

He should have known.

He should have repaired it himself.

She never would have let him.

He should have done it anyway.

He wouldn't have been able; his mind was too fractured, his body too unsteady.

He couldn't have done it.

This would have to do.

He would get used to it.

He would just have to get used to it.

Robert.

'Do you think,' Mara said just as Robert was preparing to make a roguish move on her, 'that it will just turn up one day?'

'What?' said Robert, not yet 100 per cent turned off.

'The building. Your job. Do you think it'll just turn up as if it had never been away?'

'I really have no idea how to predict potential outcomes of this scenario.'

'I mean, a sudden reappearance doesn't seem altogether outside the realm of possibility, does it?'

'An entire building I'd spent a solid chunk of my time in disappeared into the ether without leaving so much as an empty lot behind it. A reanimated dodo, who's married to a cyborg and godmother to the Mad Hatter, doesn't seem altogether outside the realm of possibility.'

Mara poked out her tongue. 'I'm sorry. I just can't figure it out. I don't know how it can have happened so I don't know how to fix it. Maybe I just have unreasonable expectations of it fixing itself.'

Robert looked away. 'Sick of having me all up in your grill?'

'No, idiot,' she said. 'Would quite like to not pay the mortgage on my own.'

'Right. Sorry. I can go back. I can check again. I should have gone back before now. I'm sorry. I'll have a look tomorrow. I've been, you know. I'm sorry.'

'I didn't mean—'

'I know. I'll have another look.'

Mara looked worried, but didn't say anything, and Robert quietly began changing into his pyjamas.

Mara didn't bring it up the next day and Robert avoided talking to her. He set out alone after lunch without mentioning to her where he was going.

He didn't listen to any music as he rode the tube. He stared at a poster for internet dating and counted stops. He felt a little clammy as he walked through the streets, one moment trudging reluctantly, the next breaking into a stride that only just escaped being a run.

He reached the street where his office was supposed to be. He turned the corner and walked down it. He reached the point on the street, and narrowly avoided melting with relief.

He let himself into the house half an hour later and walked down to Mara's office. She looked at him, biting her lip.

'I still can't find it, babe,' Robert said. 'I'm sorry.'

Mara burst into tears.

'I'm really sorry,' Robert said, moving forward, and putting his arms around her.

'No,' said Mara. 'I'm happy. Because you're so happy. I can tell, even though you feel guilty. You didn't want to find it. And I feel like you must have been unhappy there for a long time and I didn't notice, so I didn't want you to find it either, but I just don't know what we're going to do.'

Robert held her, massaging the back of her neck.

'I can keep looking for another job. I don't have references, but I can make something up to cover that.'

'No. You won't want to find one. We'll have to think of something else.'

'What will we think of?'

'I don't know. Just something.'

Robert kissed her. He kissed her for a long time.

'Later, tiger,' she said, her voice still unsteady. 'I've work to do.'

Robert kissed her one more time. And again.

Delia.

WHEN SHE FINALLY CALLED ANTHONY, Delia tried to make it sound like she wasn't lost. She hadn't wanted to call him. She didn't want to be calling him because she was lost. She wanted to be calling him because she liked his nose.

'Hello,' she said, casually, breezily, as if she were a real person, as if she were a grown up of the type with gym memberships and frequent flyer miles and other trappings of a life lived with quiet sense. 'I was thinking of having a picnic in Richmond Park. It's a lovely day. Would you care to join me?'

Delia blinked. *Care to join me.* She had said 'care to join me'.

'Oh,' said Anthony. 'All right. Would you like me to pick you up?'

'That's OK, I'm already there.'

'Ah. And where was your intended destination?'

'Oh, just a park, you know. Any park.'

There was silence.

'Victoria Park.'

'Well done,' said Anthony. 'That's kind of impressive, in a way.'

'Yes, well. Let's not get too het up about the fact that I now get lost on the tube, shall we?'

'You realise it's going to take a small eternity to get there, don't you?'

'I'll be fine waiting,' said Delia. 'I've a book.'

'Obviously that's precisely what I was worried about.'

Delia didn't read, though, while she waited. She wanted to get all her being freaked out over and done with while she was alone. It had never occurred to her that her struggle to find her way would get worse over time. That it would grow into an inability to follow clearly marked signs in tube stations, so she couldn't get on the right train.

She'd very nearly managed to rein in her panic by the time he arrived. They chatted about ordinary things like cereal preferences and talked about their days as if everything was normal. Delia told Anthony about how she'd been modelling for art classes, and how much she enjoyed Donald and Mattie and their readiness to chauffeur her the three blocks to and from her house without needing to know why. Anthony talked about the collage Jake had made of the wives of Henry VIII and how the kitchen table was now coated in glue, with tiny scraps of fabric and paper stuck to it.

There was an awkward silence while Anthony tried to make a cohesive sandwich out of torn bread and houmous he was spreading with his finger, but fortunately Delia managed to save it:

'So, what happened to your wife?' she said abruptly. It occurred to her too late that she could have led up to the subject more slowly. 'I mean, I don't know if you were married. Jake's mother. Your past co-parent.'

'My wife.'

'Right. Good. Your wife.'

'She died.'

'Oh. Um. Right.'

'There was a – thing. Jake was there. Jake found her.'

'Oh god. Um – I'm sorry. I shouldn't have brought it up.'

'It's OK. He's fine. We're fine. He's doing well.'

'Good.'

'I mean, for a kid who's lost his mother.'

'Of course.'

'His class went on a school trip to the zoo last week and he was put in charge of taking photos. Some of them are really very interesting, as well. He's good at spotting things other people miss. The teacher printed out his pictures and put them on the wall. Obviously other kids were taking photos as well, they all have phones these days, with cameras on them, but their pictures didn't get displayed because they weren't the official trip photographer.'

There was a silence while Delia tried to think of a compliment.

'Anyway,' said Anthony before she managed it, 'he's fine, he's getting along. Let's go find some deer.'

Cassie.

CASSIE HAD THOUGHT IT WOULD be nice to watch people greet each other after long absences. She knew she'd feel jealous, and she was prepared for that, but the last thing she'd expected was to be bored. But she was. Bored and dissatisfied, and even a little bit tempted to instruct people on how to greet each other.

Really, she thought, most of the reunited were quite insufficiently delighted to see each other. There were hugs and kisses, but they all could have put in a lot more effort, been a lot more rapturous. She would be rapturous.

After a few days of hard consideration, she decided the departures gate would be a much more interesting place to be stuck. It would be full of people whose excitement over going wherever they were going and why had been suddenly compromised with realisations of what and who they were leaving.

She had seen Floss off. At first there had been six months to go, which was ages, and then four, which was more than a whole season. Then six weeks, which caused a panic attack, then three, then one, and then they were there. Standing at the check-in counter, holding each other's hands so tight. Floss had barely been able to speak; Cassie couldn't keep her mouth closed.

'I think these boots were a bad choice,' Floss had said, while they stood, panicked and awkward, outside the gate to passport control. 'They're super tight.'

'But if you weren't wearing them you would've had to pack

them. They would have taken up so much room, all wedge-heeled and bulky. And this way you'll look super stylish when you get off the flight at the other end, not like most travellers. You'll look like some kind of glamorous starlet who travels all the time.'

'Yeah.'

'And you'll probably be fine. Probably feet don't swell as much as people say. I don't know, though, I've never flown for more than, like, two hours. Did your feet swell on the way over here? Or were they all right?'

'I can't remember.'

They had stood for as long as possible. They had hugged and kissed and said goodbye and then hugged and kissed again. After Floss had walked through, Cassie had stood alone for an hour.

Floss's first letter had been written from the plane. She'd spoken about the poor boy sitting next to her who hadn't known what to do about the fact that she couldn't stop crying. She'd spoken about how she could only bear to watch action movies or cartoons. How she'd been so grateful for the red wine they'd served, in spite of the fact that it was cold.

Cassie watched a young couple greet each other. They kissed briefly and walked off hand in hand. It shouldn't be brief, she thought. Kissing should never be brief.

Jake.

The rain falls like pellets on Jake's flattened and sodden hair and clothes. He shivers and waits. His mum shouldn't be taking this long. They'll be late for the doctor. Not that Jake would mind being late for the doctor, but he's worried that if they miss the doctor he won't get to go to McDonald's. Going to McDonald's is supposed to be a reward for going to the doctor.

Jake's mum wouldn't have left him standing in the rain if she'd known she was going to take this long. She doesn't even want to get the recipe she's forgotten. Jake's mum doesn't like giving other people her recipes. No one who was actually friends with Jake's mum would have asked for a recipe.

There is a flash of lightning and Jake suddenly realises how dark it's become. It shouldn't be this dark in the middle of the day. Jake squints and peers through the rain to see if she is coming.

He is just about to go in after her, to ask her if he can get changed, to show her how cold and wet he is. He is just about to move when it happens. It is sudden. It is sharp and quick. It is louder than the thunder.

Jake stands, soaked to the bone, and watches his house fall down in the rain.

No. That couldn't be it. That couldn't be it at all. His mother would have never left him standing in a thunderstorm, not even for a moment. He sighed and leaned back against a lamppost, kicking his foot against the kerb.

There was a bracelet lying in the gutter, half hidden by a leaf. Jake stood looking at it for a few minutes before he realised what It was and leaned down to pick it up. He looked around, but there was no one else on the street and, anyway, it looked like it had been there for a while.

Jake picked it up and walked on.

He came to a small grassy square and sat down, his legs crossed, the bracelet held loosely in his hand. He breathed deeply and closed his eyes. He didn't know how long he sat there for.

After some time he became aware of words being pressed into his mind. Or, rather than words, thoughts that existed before they became words and were stripped back into communicable chunks. In half-processed fragments, he was becoming aware of the history of the bracelet.

A girl had been given it by her father, the day before he left her behind. She'd worn it, in desperate hope and loneliness, for years, until one day it slipped off her wrist.

When Jake opened his eyes he felt heavy and tired. He wanted to be home. Not at his house in London, but truly home. But home was lost, he knew that.

Jake sighed, got to his feet, and left the square.

When he got back to his house, his dad wasn't there. Jake puzzled over this for a moment; his dad was almost always working in his office.

He headed up to his room, the bracelet still dangling loosely from his fingers. There were more things on the floor of his room, now. They were forming a circle around his bed, and around the map on the floor beside it, which was now dotted with symbols and the occasional words. Jake drew a silver circle on the map and placed the bracelet in the circle. He added 'Bracelet. Gutter.' to the list that now filled a quarter of an old notebook.

He looked around, looking for something else he didn't know about. He picked up an old teddy bear with a missing eye and the thin fur. He'd found it abandoned in the aisle of a supermarket. He lay on his bed, the bear clasped in one hand, and closed his eyes like before. For an age he was still, or it may have been a moment.

The same thing happened. The bear had been the favourite toy of a child who was now grown. The grown child had given it to her own daughter who had thrown it out of her pushchair without her mother noticing.

Jake picked up a pristine white satin shoe that had been dangling from the branch of a tree. A girl had had a fight with someone and tried to throw it at him. She'd missed and it had gone through the window.

Jake didn't know how long he had been in his room when he decided to go downstairs. He needed water. It took him several tries to get off his bed, and he almost fell down the stairs on his way to the kitchen.

'You look exhausted, Jake, are you OK?' his dad asked, looking up from the vegetables he was chopping.

Jake jumped. He hadn't realised his dad was there. He hadn't noticed him.

'I'm fine,' said Jake.

His dad continued making him dinner and asked him no more questions.

Marcus.

HE WAS SITTING IN THE lounge listening to her tell him about her studies. She had made them tea, a new tea she said was good, but he didn't know. He'd drunk half of his cup, but he couldn't tell whether he liked it. Her boy, that Jasper, was in the kitchen cooking dinner. Jasper wanted him to try his chilli. Did he like spicy food? Jasper had asked. He hadn't known what to say.

'He'll love it,' she'd said and Jasper had vanished but for the clashing of pans that gently echoed through from the kitchen.

She'd been talking for a while, but he was having trouble keeping track of what she was saying. He wanted to listen. He thought he was listening, but he was never sure of what she'd just said.

She'd asked him about the piano, about the new keys and he'd replied, he was sure he'd replied, but he had no idea what he'd said. He couldn't remember the last time he had said something. He wondered if he should say something.

She was looking like her mother again. He hated it when she looked like her mother. Not her mother. Her . . . there was no word. The woman.

The woman who'd auditioned a few times for Albert's theatre. The woman who'd wanted to experience pregnancy and birth, as she believed all actresses should know what it's like to give life. The woman who had not wanted the trouble or expense of raising a child. The woman who'd seemed perfect for what they wanted. The woman who'd said they could arrange everything themselves, unofficially, and she would leave them be after her part was all over.

'I'll take a year,' she'd said, sitting arrow straight, cross-legged on a chaise lounge, staring nobly into the distance. 'A year without working, without thinking about working. I'll devote myself completely to the experience of procreation.'

The woman Albert had been so thankful for.

Delia.

DELIA STOOD IMMOVABLE IN A crowd of strangers. One hand was poised in front of her lips as she gazed, wide-eyed, into the distance. Her other arm was slightly raised, as if she'd been about to point at something, but been arrested by whatever sight it was that had caught her eye.

Also, she was naked.

She was naked, and trying very hard not to think about how sore her left shoulder was. Why had her arm become so heavy? She carried it all the time, why, when she was still, did it cause such trouble?

She tried to think of something else. The eye line she'd chosen, for instance, and how she could adjust it so as not to be almost making eye contact with the balding man wearing all denim. He was working in watercolours, balding man. In murky greens and blues. Delia could see a discarded attempt out of the corner of her eye. It looked like a water nymph in an illustrated Greek myth.

She blinked.

There was a cramp in the arch of her left foot. She tried to stretch her muscles without visibly moving, but her whole leg started to shake.

'Fifteen minutes left on this pose,' said Mattie.

Delia swallowed. She swallowed her groan.

There was a tall man in the corner gesticulating wildly at his easel with a wide paintbrush. He'd finished one painting already, and taped it to the wall beside him. It was a wash of colour, with a white figure in the middle.

Beside him, a gangly girl was bent low over her paper, sketching in charcoal.

Delia's hand was going numb and she had a tickle in her throat.

By the time Mattie told her she could relax Delia almost felt like she'd never be able to move again. She got dressed behind the screen, which was thoughtfully arranged in the corner of the room, to protect her modesty she imagined. Or restore it.

Donald was waiting for her in the kitchen with a macaron that he insisted Delia eat before the ride home.

'New adventure,' he said, as she bit into it. 'Been working up to giving these a try all month. Is it all right?'

Delia assured him it was perfect, as ever, and they headed to the car.

'Not, my dear, that I don't enjoy driving you,' Donald said as he drove, 'but it can't be more than a twenty-minute walk from our house to yours. Do you have any particular aversion to journeying by foot?'

Delia was silent for a moment.

'I like walking,' she said eventually. 'I just – lately I'm not all that talented at finding my way.'

'I see.'

'No, I mean, something's actually gone horribly wrong. I never used to be like this. And now I can't get anywhere, not even the shop on the corner of my street, not even with a map. It's like I somehow forget which way to go in the second between checking it and moving.'

'Oh. How strange.'

'And I hate being such an imposition, and I'm sorry, but I'm so grateful to you as well, because I love coming to the classes.'

'Oh, it's no trouble.'

'It's a disaster,' Delia said. 'And what am I going to do? I mean, for the rest of my life, what am I going to do? I'm going to end

126

up stuck in my house, too afraid to leave it, getting everything delivered. I'll become all pasty, which is not a good look with my hair, but it won't matter because no one will ever see me because I won't be able to leave the house. It'll just be me and my mother, inside, doing needlework and snapping at each other. We'll become two little women, identical except for the fact that one's in a wheelchair and thirty years older.'

'It's going to be all right.'

'I just don't think that it is. I really don't think there's any way of this being all right. You can't get your internal compass replaced, you know. There's not some inventive medical procedure to fix this. I'm basically screwed.'

Donald pulled into the space in front of Delia's house.

'My dear,' he said, 'no matter how old we get, we somehow can never convince ourselves that whatever trial we're in the middle of is only temporary. No matter how many trials we've had in the past, and no matter how well we remember that they eventually were there no longer, we're sure that this one, this one right now, is a permanent state of affairs. But it's not. By nature humans are temporary beings.'

'You're saying I just have to ride it out until it goes away.'

'Not at all, my dear. I'm saying you have to strive for a solution and trust that eventually there will be one.'

Delia was quiet for a moment.

'Thanks for the ride,' she said. 'See you next time.'

127

Robert.

THERE'S NOTHING LIKE FORGIVENESS FOR making a person feel guilty. There's nothing like understanding for making a person feel undeserving. Because if someone is willing to forgive a weakness, they deserve better than to have to put up with it.

Robert couldn't help but feel that he was failing Mara, and her insistence that he'd done nothing wrong, that she was only concerned that he be happy, only made it worse. And the worse he felt the more he felt compelled to find a solution.

Out of guilt and worry Robert had started having a quick look for his office once a week, every Wednesday. He'd get up, go for a run, which he'd become almost good at, make his girls eggs and fruit salad, and take Bonny out for the day. Wednesdays were not for sitting in the house with books and pencils, he said, they were for getting out into the city. They were for galleries and museums and zoos and buildings. And they were for lunch or tea or a rest at any one of the many indifferent cafes that happened to be within a block or two of the street where Robert had last seen his job.

Before long, he was going more often, some weeks he would search every day. He caught up with a lot of old friends by using them as a pretext for being near where he'd last seen his job. He'd suggest places to meet nearby, pretending to himself that there was something about that particular place that he liked, and he'd wander casually down the street, trying to distract himself from his quickening heartbeat and cold hands. When he reached the nothing that had once been his building, he would feel empty and ill and exhausted.

He had stopped feeling relieved when he failed to find it; he had stopped feeling much about it at all. He would wake up anxious and try to hide it. He would go running, have breakfast, do some school work with Bonny, make lunch, and all the while he would search for an excuse to get out of the house.

He didn't try to explain to himself why his search had grown so frequent and so fearful and so fervent.

He needed to be doing better. He needed to fix it.

Mrs Featherby.

MRS FEATHERBY HAD BEEN SURPRISED by how well suited the sheet of plastic was to keeping out the rain, but it was no match for a real storm. The wind pulled at it, sending waves of agonised sound through the house and eventually the corner of the sheet pulled away from the house. Rain came streaming into her bedroom, soaking the carpet two feet into the house and splattering across the bed where she lay furious and afraid.

Knowing this was not a problem she could solve on her own, Mrs Featherby got up, swathed herself in her dressing gown and slippers and retreated to the kitchen to wait out the storm.

Bruno would tell her she was being foolish, she knew. He'd tell her to go next door and ask for help. He'd tell her that one of her neighbours would have a bed for the night. But there was no reason to take lifestyle advice from one's builder. He was performing a service for her, his chatter was incidental.

Jake.

JAKE WAS SITTING IN THE school office when he heard about the lost and found room. He was waiting to see the guidance counsellor. They were always making him see the guidance counsellor.

A girl he didn't know was talking to the office lady about a jacket she'd lost.

'It got hot the other day at lunchtime,' she was saying. 'I didn't think it was going to be hot so I put my jacket on to go to lunch. But then it did get hot, and I was sweating, so I took it off. And I forgot about it, I left it, I forgot I'd been wearing it. I forgot I'd taken it off.'

'It's OK, love,' the office lady said. 'We'll have a look for it. You come along with me to the lost and found room and we'll see if we can't find it.'

Jake watched them walk down the corridor and through a plain blue door. He chewed his lip. He didn't have to wait long for them to come back, the jacket had clearly been plainly in view. The girl clutched it to her as she left the office. Jake stared at the blue door.

'Jake?' said a voice behind him. He turned to see the counsellor standing in the doorway of her office. He got to his feet and she stepped back to let him in. She was wearing a brown jersey that was too big for her. She was always wearing clothes that were too big for her. Jake wondered if they were her husband's or her father's and she just always wore them because she never remembered to

131

buy her own clothes. Or maybe she used to be really fat and hadn't bought new clothes since she'd got thin.

'Well, Jake,' said the counsellor, when they were sitting in her office. 'How are you?'

'I'm fine, thank you,' said Jake. 'How are you?'

'I'm well. How have you been finding school this week?'

'I haven't really had to find it. It's just always been in the same place.'

The counsellor chuckled. 'Are you getting along with your classmates? Have you made many friends?'

'Yes. They're fine.'

'Well, that's good. That's really good, Jake; friends are important.'

'Yeah.'

'And how have you been feeling?'

'Fine.'

'It's OK, Jake, if you're not feeling fine. An earthquake is a big trauma to go through, even on its own, even if you hadn't lost—'

'Lots.'

'What?'

'There were lots of earthquakes. They happened for ages. They kept happening.'

'Of course. Of course. Anyway, it's hard to go through, and we can talk about it as much as you want.'

'It's fine. It was ages ago.'

'OK, well, is there anything else you want to talk about? How's your dad?'

'What?'

'Your dad. How's he doing?'

'He's fine.'

Jake sat quietly waiting for the counsellor to stop asking him questions. He sat and thought about his growing collection of lost things. He waited patiently until the counsellor told him to go.

132

Delia.

DELIA SAT ON THE FRONT step of her house watching the two girls who were probably not twelve have an argument. It seemed that the one with long hair had brought home a boy the one with tiny feet had wanted. Delia wondered why they weren't waiting until they were inside for their recriminations. When did the world become so public? The one with all the flowing locks, who was holding a set of keys in front of her, appeared to think of a new point every time she went to unlock the door, so Delia got to hear every 'you knew how I felt' and every 'you're just trying to make Gerald jealous'. At least it sounded like Gerald, but Delia didn't really think there were still actual people called Gerald, so it may have been something else.

Finally, Anthony walked up the street towards her.

'Hello,' said Delia, jumping up. 'What shall we do?'

Anthony looked at her for a moment before speaking. 'So, here's a thing,' he said. 'My son has lost his accent. I think it happened ages ago, slowly enough that I didn't realise it. And then this morning he said, "If I have a bowl of cereal will there be enough milk? We've run out of bread." And I realised that his accent is completely gone. He might have lived here all his life.'

'Oh,' said Delia. 'Is that bad?'

'Probably not. I don't know. It was inevitable, I suppose, that he'd end up sounding British. I'm surprised I haven't started to, too. It's just that he doesn't sound like his mother anymore, you

133

see. He doesn't have her tricks of speech anymore. Bound to happen. No way to stop it.'

Delia looked away and back again. 'Well, thanks. That was a great start to the night. Set the mood brilliantly.' She blinked, suddenly ashamed. 'Sorry. I shouldn't be sarcastic about your motherless child.'

'It's OK. I should have led with a pithy anecdote.'

'Well. We'll both know for next time, I suppose.'

'Live and let learn. No, wait, that's not it.'

'Moving on, I think the answer to my earlier question is "take some wine to the park and drink too much of it". OK?'

'Yeah, go on.'

Delia narrowed her eyes and smiled.

Being drunk in a park isn't quite like being drunk anywhere else. It doesn't have the tawdry dimness of a pub or the deafening beats of a club. You can be expansive without being an arse, you can marvel at the few stars still visible through the light pollution, you can gambol and frolic. Delia had lost track of how long she'd been talking for. She always forgot she was a loquacious drunk until it was too late.

She was sitting precariously in a tree and telling Anthony earnestly about how she was finding sitting for art classes; she couldn't tell whether he was listening, which really didn't matter to her at this stage. Not being listened to is no reason not to talk, if you feel like talking. He was humming what sounded like a Disney song.

'I've been very proud of myself actually, for caring so little about the cellulite on my thighs and the scar on my belly.'

Anthony stopped humming.

'What?'

'Well, you know. I always think I shouldn't mind about things like that, but I always actually do mind. But I haven't. I'm all, "Here is my body. Look at it. Look at it, and draw. Draw like the wind." It's incredibly mature of me.'

134

'Sorry,' said Anthony, swallowing. 'You weren't, um, naked, were you?'

'Yeah. Of course. That's what life modelling is, right? You draw, don't you? You know.'

'I draw buildings. That don't exist yet.'

'Well, fine. Well, this is art, you know. Life drawing. And it's kind of surprised even me, to be honest; I never would have done this kind of thing when I was young and crazy.' Delia stopped talking for a moment. Anthony hadn't started humming again. 'Are you OK?,' she asked.

'Fine. I'm fine. I just didn't realise that's what you'd be doing.'

'Right. Are you upset about it?'

'No. Of course not.'

'Right.'

Delia looked down carefully, placed one hand on the trunk of the tree, and one on the branch she was sitting on, and attempted to ease herself off. She stumbled a little and grazed her arm on the tree.

'Ow,' she said. 'Let's go back. You lead.' She stared at Anthony, waiting for him to turn towards the street so she knew which way she was going. 'I'm quite good at it, you know. I have very strong legs. Apparently lots of them can't do standing poses for longer than ten minutes, but I can make it for at least twenty. Probably more if I had to. I'm that good. Although, although, last time, there was this one pose, the last one, and it was, ooh, maybe forty-five minutes, right, and I was lying down, but I had one arm under my head. Actually, it wasn't really under my head, it was just flung up beside it, and kind of falling backwards. Anyway, for the last ten minutes it was completely numb. Not in a painless "it's best you don't know what's happening to your arm right now" kind of way, more like a "what are you doing, this isn't natural, I don't know how to handle it, so I'm saving all this pain for later, but I am going to hit you with it hard in a bit" kind of way. But anyway, the teacher likes me, so she's asked me back a couple of times, and her husband drives me there and back home so I don't get lost.'

They were walking down her street and she knew that she was talking almost as loudly as the shouty girls across the road, but she didn't care.

'Well,' said Anthony when they got to her house. 'I guess I'll see you later.'

'Nope, you're coming upstairs.'

'What?'

'Pfft,' said Delia. 'Come the fuck on.'

She opened the door and walked upstairs without checking whether he was following.

'Right,' she said, forty-seven seconds later as he closed her bedroom door. She kicked off her shoes and pulled off her dress.

'What are you doing?' said Anthony.

'You're jealous.' She unhooked her bra. 'Of all the strange artists who get to see me naked. It's stupid, and you shouldn't be, but you are.'

'No, I'm not.'

'Bullshit, dickhead.'

He said nothing. She pulled down her knickers and kicked them away.

'Anyway, so now you can draw me if you want. You draw.'

He cleared his throat. 'I draw buildings.'

'Yes, that don't exist. But that's for work. This is for leisure, no?'

She stood in front of him, arms akimbo. 'This pose isn't my best work, to be honest, but you're not paying me, so that's what you get.'

'Um,' said Anthony.

'Fine, you don't have to draw me if you don't want to.'

'OK.'

'You should do something though. With me, I mean.'

'Right.'

Delia waited a moment. 'Anytime.'

'It's just a bit weird, isn't it? You're already naked.'

'Well, I'm not getting dressed again just so you can make a move.'

'Right. Fair enough.'

He took a couple of steps forward. He put his hands on her shoulders, then moved them to her face, then back to her shoulders. He leaned forward and kissed her. After that, things moved a lot faster. Suspiciously fast.

'Oh hell,' said Delia as Anthony knocked over her lamp trying to get his jeans off. 'This is, isn't it, since she, your, this is the first time you've, oh hell.'

'Shit. I should have said.'

'No, you shouldn't, you just shouldn't have made it so bloody obvious. I really would have preferred not to know. Ah well. Let's carry on, shall we?'

'Did I break the lamp, do you think?'

'I don't care.'

Delia crawled backwards onto the bed and dragged Anthony with her. He seemed to be spending a lot of time around her face. 'I've got boobs, you know,' she said.

'Right. They're lovely, by the way.'

Once he'd dived below the shoulder line Anthony seemed to find his stride a bit better. She hadn't really thought they'd get to this point, or at least not so quickly, but it was a lot more fun than hiking around London's forgotten suburbs. Anthony was clumsy, and clearly out of practice, but as he pushed into her, his enthusiasm made up for it.

He certainly seemed happy by the end. He sighed happily as he lay back on the bed and pulled her to his chest. They lay still for a long time.

'Sorry,' he said after a bit. 'I was almost asleep for a moment there.'

'Well it's probably a good idea for you to get some rest before you have to scale my fire escape so my mum doesn't find out I'm no longer pure.'

'What?'

'Joke, loser.'

'Right.'

'Actually, you should probably go home soon, no? Jake's still a little young to have the house to himself overnight, isn't he?'

'Who?'

'What do you mean? Jake. Your son. Jake.'

Suddenly Anthony looked pale.

'Oh god,' he said. 'I'm sorry. I shouldn't – I'm sorry.'

'What?' asked Delia. 'It's OK. Of course you can't stay over. It's fine.'

'No, I just –' He'd started getting dressed and he wasn't looking at her. 'Um, I'll see you later, OK?'

Delia watched him go, feeling unnerved. Then she slowly started rearranging the bedding into a more sleep-appropriate format. Probably he'd just been worried at being out so late with Jake on his own. She curled up tight and went to sleep.

Robert.

'ROB,' HIS MARA SAID TO him when he walked in the door one night after going for a drink with a friend he'd neither seen, nor wanted to see, since he was at university.

'Yeah, hon?' he said.

'Can you do me a favour, please?'

'Sure.'

'I know it's hard, but I really think you should try. Can you please stop looking for your job? Can you please let it go? Please stop beating yourself up like this.'

Robert was silent. He took off his jacket and hung it up.

The Notebook.

ITEM: NOTEBOOK
Place found: London Zoo Lost and Found.

The notebook was once the most important possession of a fourteen-year-old boy. He kept the notebook in his back pocket. He'd had it for eight months and in it he wrote down things he saw. Sometimes they were brief, single phrases to capture a fleeting moment. Sometimes they were a couple of pages long, and these were usually people. With people, he liked to put down as much detail as possible. He had no plan for the notebook, it was just something he liked to do.

He lost it when he was lying around in Regents Park with a girl. With *the* girl – as a girl always is when you're fourteen. She was pretty and she blinked at him and for two hours he forgot to check his back pocket as obsessively as usual. At the end of the two hours, he was in line for movie tickets with his friends and the notebook had been picked up by the last person to be described in it. The girl.

She was scared by how closely he'd described her and offended by his mention of her freckles and her slightly crooked nose and she tore those pages to pieces before throwing the whole notebook away.

Robert.

ROBERT FELT A LITTLE LIKE he was addicted. Like he was going through withdrawal. In all his unoccupied moments he would find his mind drifting towards the tube station, descending into the bowels of London's public transport, trundling through tunnels and stations and emerging into the heart of the city to wander along streets he knew so well, until it arrived at the point that had so suddenly become so inexplicably alien to him. When his mind went there alone it arrived at nothing, at a white space void of memory. He wondered at this; he could picture the street as it used to be and as it was now easily enough, but somehow both were lost by the end of his mental journey. Every time he got there, to that blankness, he grew panicked and desperate. He forgot, in his distance, which was the reality and which the memory, and on his worst days, began almost to believe in the void.

He had promised Mara he wouldn't go back. He knew she wouldn't ask again, and it was because he knew this that he was so determined. And yet, surely just checking once more would be better. Just making sure one more time would do more good than harm, wouldn't it? It would be better than not knowing. Not that he didn't know, but double-checking was always wise.

He began to wonder if there was a time he could make a trip in without upsetting anyone. He was sure it would be better, it would stop him being so moody, it would mean he could move on. He'd be able to concentrate more on teaching Bonny, he'd be

better to Mara. Going to look for his work again would be a
solution, not a problem.

But he had promised. She had begged him and he had promised.

He stayed quiet about it, but he kept thinking. Every day it
crossed his mind more often.

Mrs Featherby.

Mrs Featherby had not heard from Bruno, the builder who had seemed so nice, in more than two weeks. She was growing used to the gentle rippling of her plastic wall, but she was not quite able to accustom herself to the feeling that her entire life was on show to all who walked by.

Indeed, this open style of living had caused a development that Mrs Featherby was not fully prepared for. She was to have a visitor.

It was a Sunday afternoon and she was expecting Small Girl Bonny for tea. She had spoken to the child, or rather the child had spoken to her, almost every day, but this was her first formal visit. Mrs Featherby had worried for a time about what was suitable to feed a tiny girl, but in the end she decided to stick with what she knew. She had a strict policy of always having a cake or loaf on hand for these kinds of social occasions, although fortunately she'd seldom needed to use them.

Small Girl Bonny, as Mrs Featherby was referring to her in order to differentiate between her and a rather large woman named Bonny she'd known forty-odd years earlier, was due to show up at 3.53pm. The two of them had had a serious discussion on the topic of time, and mutually agreed. It suited both Mrs Featherby's conviction that three was too early and five too late, and Bonny's passion for palindromes. She didn't know they were palindromes, despite Mrs Featherby's earnest attempt to explain, she just thought they were funny.

Mrs Featherby was placing small sandwiches on a plate when she heard a small voice pronounce a hesitant hello from the garden. She pursed her lips. Despite not having had a front door for several weeks now, she could not get used to people hailing her in this fashion. She knew she couldn't really ask for a more appropriate announcement, especially from a child, but it remained galling nonetheless.

'Hello Small Girl Bonny,' she said to the outline of a child on her sitting-room wall. 'Would you like to come in?'

'Um, what's the time, please?' said the outline.

'Currently it is 3.49pm.'

'Oh. OK. I'll have to wait then.'

'It's quite all right, you can come in now,' said Mrs Featherby. The childish silhouette stood still for a moment. 'Um,' it began. 'Maybe not. Maybe I'll wait.'

'Well, if that's what you'd prefer.'

'Can you please just tell me when it's the right time?'

'Certainly I can,' said Mrs Featherby. She returned to the plate of sandwiches, placing them on a tray with the teapot and cups. She carried them through to the sitting room and then seated herself quietly to wait out the final minute.

As soon as the clock ticked over to 3.53pm exactly, she crossed to the small figure outlined in the plastic.

'Is that you, Small Girl Bonny?' she said to it. 'What impeccable timing you have. Won't you come in?'

She pulled back the opening that was serving for a door and for the first time saw her tiny neighbour in sharp relief.

Her beam transformed to an uncertain grimace as she stared into the depths of the sitting room and up at Mrs Featherby.

Mrs Featherby put out her hand to be shaken.

'How do you do, Small Girl Bonny,' she said.

'Um, good,' she replied, blinking.

'How excellent to hear. If you'd like to take a seat over on the sofa, I shall pour you some tea.'

144

'OK.' Small Girl Bonny strode across the room in an unexpectedly decisive manner and perched herself on Mrs Featherby's brocade sofa. Mrs Featherby sat opposite her and poured them each a cup of tea, adding a slice of lemon to her own and plenty of milk to Bonny's.

They sipped in silence.

'My mum says I shouldn't bother you so much. She says I should leave you alone because you are so sad.'

'Why does your mother think I'm sad?' asked Mrs Featherby, startled.

'Because. Can I have a sandwich?'

'Certainly you may have a sandwich.' She put a few on a plate for Bonny and placed it carefully on the table in front of her. 'What does your father think about you coming here?'

'He said to not break anything.'

'I see your father is a practical man.'

'He's a wizard.'

'Of course he is.'

Mrs Featherby picked out a sandwich for herself. She took a small bite and chewed carefully.

'So you don't think I'm sad, Small Girl Bonny?' she asked.

'I don't know. You're not crying. Are you sad?'

Mrs Featherby thought for a moment. 'I don't know either,' she said.

'Why do you live here all alone and no one ever comes to visit you and you never go to visit anyone and you are here all alone?'

Mrs Featherby thought for another moment.

'Would you like a slice of cake?'

'Yes.'

Mrs Featherby cut off two slices of cake and placed one on Small Girl Bonny's plate. The other she set down in front of herself.

'You want to know why I'm alone?' she asked.

'All right,' said the girl, through a mouthful of cake.

'Well,' began Mrs Featherby, 'I suppose that for a very long time I wasn't really allowed to make friends. And then after a while I was again, but I'd forgotten how to do it.'

'Why weren't you allowed to make friends?'

'It was part of my job for a while.'

'It was your job to not have friends?'

'In a manner of speaking.'

Small Girl Bonny chewed. She crammed the rest of the cake into her mouth and chewed some more.

'What was your job?' she asked.

Mrs Featherby regarded her guest carefully for a moment.

'Now,' she said, leaning forwards. 'I can tell you, Small Girl Bonny, but I have to know that I can trust you first.'

'OK,' said the child.

'So you can't tell your mother or your father or your friends.'

'OK.' Small Girl Bonny rubbed her nose, smearing jam across her cheek.

'Well,' said Mrs Featherby, who was feeling more like Wendy than she had in years, 'I used to be a spy.'

'A spy?'

'A spy.'

'Like James Bond?'

'What do you know about James Bond?'

'He wears a suit all the time and drinks mint tea. My dad told me a story about him. There was a king who could turn things to gold but he did it to a real live girl, which wasn't very nice because then the girl stopped being a real live girl and started being a real dead girl.'

'Ah. That classic tale.'

'Were you famous?' said the girl, her eyes suddenly wide.

'Well, spies can't really be famous, Small Girl Bonny. They have to be secret. No one can know who they are, you see, which is why having friends is difficult for them.'

'Oh.' Bonny seemed to consider this for a moment. 'Why did you stop being a spy?'

146

'You don't exactly stop being a spy, actually, not officially. But it's been many years since I've been given an assignment, so I don't think I'm really needed anymore.'

'Was it evil spies that took the front of your house away?'

'I don't think so.'

'But how do you know?' Small Girl Bonny looked serious.

'Because there aren't really any evil spies. There are spies who work for different countries, countries that disagree about things and want to know what each other are doing in case one of the things they disagree about makes them want to fight each other.'

'Oh. How do you become a spy?'

'It's different for everyone, I imagine, but this is how I became one. I was nineteen and my parents had both died suddenly, within weeks of each other, and I had to get a job. So I started working in a bookshop, and two men, who hadn't come in together, started talking. One of them asked the other if he liked *Hard Times*, which is a book you should read one day. The other man said, 'Yes, I like it enormously. I read it for the first time when I was seventeen and I read it again last year,' which is a perfectly normal thing to say, except that it wasn't true. He was lying, and I knew he was lying. I didn't know how I knew, but I did. After the first man had left the second man came up to buy a newspaper and I asked him why he'd lied about reading *Hard Times*. He asked how I knew he was lying and I said I just knew.'

Small Girl Bonny was sitting on her hands and swinging her legs as she gazed silently at Wendy Featherby.

'A week or two later the second man came back and he asked about all sorts of different people who had been into the shop and whether or not they'd lied to me. Now I'd noticed quite a few people saying stupid things that weren't true to me, things that there were no reason to lie about, so naturally I remembered them. But I also remembered all the people he asked about who hadn't lied, and he was very impressed with that.'

'So he asked you if you wanted to be a spy?' asked Small Girl Bonny.

'He did. And I said no, and he asked again, and I wasn't really enjoying the bookshop so much, so I said yes.'

'So, if I want to be a spy I should get a job in a bookshop?'

'Perhaps you want to think about it for a few years before you decide you want to be a spy.'

'Well, OK,' said the girl. 'Will you tell me stories about it?'

'Maybe one day,' Mrs Featherby said, rising and putting the crumb-laden plates back on the tray. 'I think you've heard quite enough for now.'

'Is it time for me to go home?'

'Almost definitely.'

'Can I please come again, please?'

'If you like.'

'OK.'

Mrs Featherby walked Small Girl Bonny to the makeshift door and shook her hand in farewell. She watched her amble over the road to her house and have her hair tousled by the man who was waiting by the front door, and then she pinned her plastic sheet back in place. She carried the tray of tea things back to her kitchen and silently began to wash up.

Jake.

JAKE PLANNED IT VERY CAREFULLY. He took his mum's old glasses from his dad's office. They hadn't really been his mum's glasses. They had belonged to his grandfather and his mum had always liked to have them around. His dad had kept them sitting on top of a small shelf, along with a necklace and a diary.

He started wearing the glasses to school. He couldn't wear them for long, because they made his eyes hurt, so when he had to take them off he hooked them in the front of his shirt. When people asked about them, he said, 'My mum used to do this. They were her father's glasses,' and then they usually stopped asking.

After a couple of weeks, he slipped out of school at lunchtime and placed the glasses under a pile of leaves around the corner, where no one could see him.

That afternoon, in class, just before the teacher was about to start a spelling test, Jake put up his hand.

'I've lost my glasses,' he said. 'My grandfather's glasses. I've lost the glasses my mum left.'

'Oh dear,' said his teacher. 'Has anyone seen Jake's glasses?' The class mutely shook its collective head. 'Jake, dear, you'd better go to the office and see if they've been handed in.'

Jake hid his smile and left the classroom. He walked alone down the corridor that led to the front of the school and the office.

The office lady was very concerned about his glasses. Jake guessed that the teacher or the counsellor had told her they were his mother's. She took him straight to the blue door and led him through it.

The room was not big, and it was not as full as Jake had thought it would be, but there were still a lot of things. The walls were lined with cheap wooden shelves, which were littered with an assortment of childish possessions. There were a lot of jerseys and jackets, some books, a few toys.

'Now, precious, no one brought a pair of glasses to me, but I did go on a break for a while and they may have been handed in then. Can you see them anywhere?'

'Not yet,' said Jake, 'but I'll have a good look.'

'You do that, love. I should really go through the lot of it and make a list. Set it up so that as soon as something is turned in we write it down. Then organise this room so that you know where to look for a specific thing. I just get so busy. There's always something new cropping up just when I think I'm about to get a bit of time.'

'I could do that, if you like,' Jake said quickly. 'I could help. I could start now.'

'Oh, you are just too sweet. We'll see, shall we? Now, are you OK to have a look by yourself? I've a pile of things to get on with.'

Jake nodded and waited for her to leave. She left the door open, but Jake pushed it closed after her. For a moment he just stood in the middle of the room, looking at the shelves. The small things, he decided, as he didn't have his bag with him.

There was a pen lying half under an old cardigan. It was silver and heavy, not the kind of pen a school kid would use. Jake picked it up quickly. He knew he should wait till he got home, but he couldn't. He closed his eyes.

By the time he left the room, he had five things in his pockets and he was exhausted.

'Heavens,' said the office lady when he walked past her. 'I'd completely forgotten you were in there, my love. Did you find them?'

'No,' said Jake. 'They're not in there.'

'Oh, precious. I'm sorry. But they might turn up, you know. Someone might hand them in yet. I'll keep a special eye out for you, how about that?'

'Thanks,' said Jake. He was trying desperately to keep his eyes open.

'Are you all right, love? You look rather pale.'

'I'm OK. No, I feel a bit sick. Can I go home, do you think?'

'I'm sure that's fine, precious. I'll send a message to your teacher.'

Jake had left his bag in his class but he didn't want to go all the way back to get it. It would still be there tomorrow, after all; the teacher would look after it. He left the school and walked around the corner.

He went to get the glasses from their hiding place. The street had been swept. The glasses were gone.

Cassie.

THE BARK WAS NOW ABOUT the height of a pair of low-rider jeans. Strangely, it was becoming more comfortable. Cassie wasn't sure if it was because she was growing used to it or because her weight was now supported by wood instead of muscle and bone.

For once, she and her mother were having a rest from each other. For the first time in weeks, her mother had left the airport, although she'd promised to be back within a couple of hours. Cassie's best friend, Bridie, had finally shown up and convinced her mother to go home for a while. She dragged a set of four connected chairs over next to Cassie, greeting the protests of the airport staff with a wide-eyed 'My best friend is turning into a tree', with which they could hardly argue.

She sat cross-legged on the last of the seats staring at Cassie's feet.

'I didn't believe you, you know,' she said. 'I mean, of all the people I know, you are probably the most likely to turn into a tree, but I didn't believe you'd actually started doing it.'

'What do you mean, I'm the mostly likely person to turn into a tree?'

'You can't really argue with that now, can you? So, you just decided to park it here? You're ready to put down roots?'

'Stop it.'

'I will not. But I'm sorry. I'm sorry it took me this long. I didn't want to have to stop not believing you were turning into a tree. Or something.'

'It's fine,' said Cassie. 'I've been fine.'

'Well, I'm still sorry. Anyway, I can't believe you're getting this extreme over that Floss girl.'

'When did she become "that Floss girl"? I thought you liked her?'

'Sure, she was fine. I don't know. I'm a bit jealous, I suppose.'

'You have a boyfriend.'

'I know, and it's not like if I didn't have a boyfriend, I'd be keen on the ladies. I just thought that if you were ever going to go for a girl, I would be the girl you'd go for. But you've never even tried to kiss me, not even when you've been really drunk.'

'Do you want me to hit on you?'

'Oh no, please. That would be super awkward. I'm not even a little bit not straight.'

'I know.'

'Good.'

Cassie laughed. Then she stopped laughing. She hadn't laughed in days. She shouldn't be laughing. She'd lost her lover. There were times you shouldn't laugh.

'Thank Christ I've got a laugh out of you. You should never not be laughing.'

'What?'

Bridie had taken off her shoes and started painting her toenails orange. 'You laugh. It's what you do. It's how you respond to almost every social situation. You are The Girl Who Laughs. When we had that huge argument over Darryn Coates, before you realised you were a vagetarian, even when you were trying to yell at me you were laughing.'

Cassie wondered if she could convince Bridie to paint her fingernails. Normally Bridie hated doing other people's make-up or hair or anything like that, but she might do Cassie's fingernails, considering they were the only nails Cassie had left.

'Then,' Bridie went on, 'when that Floss was leaving, you didn't laugh so much anymore. It wasn't like you were mopey or anything, you just didn't laugh as often, or much at all. It's been really annoying. And it's even more annoying now in, like, retrospect, when it turns out that it was all for some strumpet who can't even be bothered to let you know why she wasn't on the plane she was supposed to be on.'

'Probably that's why she's the right one. If she's the only one who can stop me laughing all the time.'

'Well, in the first place, you're only just twenty, you hardly know that she's the only one that can do that, and in the second, that's totally stupid because why would you want to be with someone who makes you stop laughing? The right one is the one that makes you happy. That is all.'

'Whatever. Jerm doesn't make you happy. You're always complaining about him.'

'Jerm drives me the craziest. Do you know he eats toast with just pickled onions on it? I have to kiss that mouth, and he shows it no respect. But actually, he does make me happy. None of the stupid things he does really stop him making me happy. So there.'

'Well, Floss makes me happy.'

'She didn't. She made you anxious and insecure.'

Cassie decided not to ask Bridie to paint her nails. It was a stupid colour anyway, orange. Who would want orange nails? Cassie wanted pinks and pearly off-whites. Bridie was always too brightly coloured.

'You don't have to stay if you don't want to,' she said, folding her arms so her hands were hidden.

'I do too,' said Bridie. 'Because, a, I promised your mum, and b, I actually miss you. You don't get to just stop hanging out with me because you're all piney over the strumpet and stuck to the floor. I brought my laptop so we can watch *Back to the Future* if you want. And I have a bunch of books for you, as well, that I have to tell you why you will like before I let you read them. Also, I have things going on that I've had to talk to you about in my imagination and it's just not any good.'

'No,' said Cassie. 'I'm annoyed with you. You're being completely blasé about my having lost the love of my life. Who, I'm finding out for the first time, you didn't even like.'

'OK, number one, princess, we stopped believing in the loves of our lives when we were seventeen; number two, I didn't not like her, I just thought you were too much of a different person because of her; and number three, I'm allowed to be blasé about your having lost her if you're going to be blasé about the tree you're turning into.'

'That makes no sense.'

'It does and I don't care if it doesn't.'

Bridie had finished her toenails. She had her feet slung over the arm of the seat with her toes splayed apart. It had always made Cassie feel ill, the way Bridie could splay her toes like that. She could keep them like that for ages; they made Cassie think of monkeys.

'Should I do my fingers to match,' she was asking, 'or should I do them blue?'

Delia.

DELIA WAS LOST, AGAIN, OF course, but this time it was with Anthony so it was a lot more interesting.

They'd been walking along the South Bank until Delia had decided they should cross the road and turn left. After an hour walking they were halfway down a street of council estates, and Delia's feet would have been very sore had Anthony not been so fascinating.

He'd told her old stories of school, of being the interesting British student at university, of buildings he'd designed. The only thing he hadn't talked about was his son.

'How's Jake?' Delia asked after a while. She suddenly wondered when Anthony had last mentioned Jake; she didn't think he had in a few days.

'What?' Anthony replied. He was understandably taken aback, given that he'd been in the middle of telling her about the time he'd run over his dad's dog when he was seventeen.

'You haven't talked about Jake in a while.'

'Jake.'

'Yes.'

Anthony looked confused for a moment. 'Oh. I don't know,' he said finally. 'He's fine I think.'

'Good. School going well?' She didn't know why the conversation suddenly felt so awkward.

'Oh, yes, seems to be. How's your mum?'

'My mum? She's fine. She ordered a new sampler pattern. It's three metres wide and every evening I have to stretch it out so she can see how much she's done. Which, so far, is about four-inches square.'

'Has she minded you being out of the house so much?'

'I think she's enjoyed it, to be honest. She actually had a friend over the other day, first time in years. Makes me almost feel that I've been in the way all these years, instead of helping her out.'

'Maybe she's just liked finding out that she's not as dependent as she thought she was.'

'Well, I haven't liked finding I'm much more dependent than I should be.'

'Come on, this isn't so bad. We would never have seen this row of houses.'

'That is true. We are fortunate indeed.'

'And if she finds she doesn't need you so much, you can think about what you want to do.'

'What?'

'Well, you can get back to what you were doing before the accident.'

'Oh. Right.'

'What were you doing? You've never told me.'

'Oh, I was studying. Doing my master's.'

There was a silence.

They walked.

'Is there a particular reason you don't want to talk about it?' asked Anthony.

'What? I don't not want to talk about it.'

'OK. What was it in, your master's?'

If left unused, conversations can grow rusty over time. The opinions and feelings we've expressed before, when left to their own devices, can grow sluggish and curmudgeonly. They become too used to sitting alone and unconsidered, and if you ask them to move, their joints can ache, or parts of them can crumble away.

Sometimes you can return to an opinion you've not visited in years and find it's died and rotted away without you even noticing. Sometimes a feeling we assume we'll have for ever can abandon us and leave a gap we don't notice until we suddenly feel the need to call upon that feeling.

Delia had talked about her plan more often than most people talk about the weather. She'd thought about it so often that it was there, just under her tongue, to be brought out on the slightest excuse. She wanted to paint, for ever, but she didn't want to just do that. She didn't want to lock herself up in a studio and paint, all alone, all the time, because people who did that got bored and lonely and crotchety and crazy and cut off their own ears, which didn't have anything to do with being a genius, she didn't care what people said. She wanted to be an art seller as well as a painter. She wanted to have a small gallery, and she wouldn't display any of her own work, because that would be self-indulgent, and there were too many self-indulgent artists already, and she was bored of them. She would have a gallery and she would find exciting people that no one had heard of and she would tell everyone why they had to like them and pay thousands of pounds for their work. Her own paintings would have to find other galleries to be displayed in.

But she had closed the door of her old bedroom and now her life conversation was stiff and prone to complaining.

'Art,' Delia said. 'It was in fine arts.'

Marcus.

DAYS HAD ALWAYS HAD STRUCTURE for him. Light breakfast, music, full breakfast, read the paper, call Katharine, go for a walk, lunch, music, write letters, dinner, read, bed. Simple, but what he liked.

It should be easy to keep it so, he thought. Even on days when he couldn't bring himself to go into the music room, couldn't bring himself to touch the alien keys that were not a part of his piano. The keys that were not a part of him. He should still be able to keep to the rest. The rest could continue as it was.

Except it couldn't. He didn't know why, but he couldn't make it continue as it was. His life couldn't continue as it was.

He found himself standing, he never knew how long for, unsure of what he was supposed to do next. He could no longer be certain even of when, or if, he was hungry or thirsty.

Shouldn't be this hard, he thought. Easy things to know, these are. You just know. And then you just do something about it.

He didn't know anymore. He couldn't tell. She would come over to check on him in the evenings and ask if he'd eaten and he wouldn't be sure. He couldn't say for certain. He should lie, he thought, so she didn't worry. He didn't want her to worry. But he could never remember to lie until it was too late.

He had to make it better. He had to try harder for it to be better.

Cassie.

Cassie was staring at Bridie.

'You look really good.'

Bridie appeared not to notice the sudden change of topic.

'Thanks. I try.'

'Your hair's all shiny.'

'It's always shiny.'

'No, it's not. It's crazy and fluffy and full of split ends.'

'Cassie!'

'Now it's not. Now it's like it's almost glowing. And your skin looks amazing as well.'

'No more than usual. I've always had good skin.'

But it was more than usual. Bridie wasn't wrong about her skin, but more than looking good, it looked luminous. And her eyes were brighter and, although Cassie couldn't tell this just by looking at her, she hadn't broken a nail in three weeks. Bridie rarely got through a day without a nail breaking or tearing a cuticle.

It took Cassie a day or two to notice, but it wasn't just Bridie, either. Everyone Cassie saw was looking like they'd just returned from a month at a health retreat. People stood near her for five minutes after a missed connection and two long-haul flights and felt suddenly renewed, as if they'd just woken up in cool linen sheets, after the deepest sleep of their lives.

There was one exception.

Cassie's mother was looking haggard and deflated. Her hair was becoming grizzled and her face was creased and sagging. Somehow even her clothes were looking grey and lifeless.

That was the one development Cassie didn't notice.

Mrs Featherby.

THE DAY WAS WARM AND Mrs Featherby was outside. She was outside, walking. While this was not in itself altogether unusual, her experience of it was markedly different to previous walks. Where before she would have enjoyed a solitary stroll with just the barest of acknowledgements of people she passed along the way, now that was no longer possible. People stopped to chat, whether she wanted them to or not.

One of the young girls so given to being inappropriately dressed stopped Mrs Featherby to ask how long she was going to have to wait for her wall and went on to chat about the boy she'd started seeing. With wide eyes she described how embarrassed she was when he came to her house, as he was very neat and neither she nor her flatmate were particularly good at keeping the house tidy.

She was lying. Her flatmate tried to keep it tidy but was unable to counter the mess the girl knew she was ever spreading forth.

She was lying and Mrs Featherby knew it.

The blustery old man who lived around the corner asked her how she was keeping warm and whether it wasn't disgraceful that she'd been kept waiting as long as she had. He ranted contentedly for several minutes on the insufficiencies of your average tradesman. He told an extended fallacy about a time a plumber had pretended to fix the bathroom sink while actually stealing the taps and replacing them with similar, but inferior fittings.

Lying had once been such a surprise to Mrs Featherby, back when she was a very young Wendy. Until she could hear the lies everywhere she had assumed most people to be honest. She hadn't started believing people were honest again, over the long years of her solitude, but she'd forgotten just how often and how needlessly they lied.

When Mrs Featherby got back to her garden, she found someone waiting for her.

'Good afternoon, Small Girl Bonny,' she said.

'I yelled four times but you didn't hear me,' said the child.

'No. Well, I've been out, you see.'

'Oh. OK.'

'And how are you today?'

'Oh, I'm OK, I suppose.'

'Just OK, my dear?'

'I think my dad is sad.'

'Why do you think that?'

'I just think it. He used to go to work all of the time. And then he didn't and it was really fun and he taught me my school.'

'And he doesn't do that anymore?'

'No, he still does but now it's not so fun because I think he's sad.'

'Sometimes people do get sad for a bit, but usually they come round.'

'Oh.' The girl started chewing the end of her hair.

'My mum says will you come for dinner please?' she said.

Mrs Featherby pursed her lips and looked across the street to Small Girl Bonny's house for a moment.

'Thank you, Small Girl Bonny,' she said. 'That's a very kind invitation, but I think not. I'm afraid I have,' she paused for a moment. 'I have some things I must attend to.'

'Oh. OK,' said the girl. 'I have to go now, it's my job to set the table.'

Mrs Featherby watched the small figure run over to her house. She walked inside and headed to her kitchen where she contemplated what to prepare herself for a solitary dinner.

Robert.

ROBERT WAS SITTING BY THE window one Friday afternoon, after his lessons with Bonny were over. He was sitting quietly, barely moving, when Mara walked in with an expression on her face like she was bearding a lion in a particularly unpleasant den rather than addressing a quite ordinary man in her own lounge.

'Why don't you clear out the shed?' she said. 'And stop bothering me.'

'How am I bothering you? I'm not doing anything.'

'You're bothering me. You're sitting in here all still and moody and obsessing over things and it's seeping through the walls. Please, just give me an hour of knowing you're healthily distracted. Clear out the shed.'

'We have a shed?' said Robert. 'Since when?'

'It's always been there. When we moved in you said you'd clear it out one day and do something with it. You never had time. Now you do.'

'Right. OK. Sure.'

The first problem, when he got out there, was the darkness. The windows of the shed were large but covered with grime. Robert flicked the switch that was set onto the wall. Nothing happened. He squinted up to the set of three naked bulbs that were set in a triangle on the ceiling.

'Right,' he said. He walked back into the house.

'Babe,' he said, poking his head round Mara's office door.

'Yes?'

'The lights are out.'

'Do we have more bulbs?'

'Right. Probably.'

'Good.'

'Right.'

He went through to the kitchen and rummaged around. There were only two, but he decided that would do for now. He dragged a kitchen chair outside with him and changed two of the bulbs. He flicked the switch again. He looked around.

'Hon,' Robert stepped into Mara's office again.

'Yes,' said Mara, a little too sweetly.

'There's all this wood.'

'What?'

'In the shed. There's heaps of wood.'

'Well. That's what needs clearing out, tiger.'

'But I think – it seems quite good.'

'Good?'

'The wood. I think it's good wood. Oak or something, I think.'

'So?'

'So maybe we should use it for something.'

'Like what?'

'I don't know. Something. Maybe I should make some stuff with it.'

Mara turned around in her chair.

'Did you take woodwork in school? Do you know how to safely use power tools?'

'I think so.'

'OK. Knock yourself out.' She turned back to her work.

Robert stood for a while staring at the giant pile of dark wood. He wasn't really sure what to make, but he was sure he wanted to make something. It was the most sure he'd been about anything in months. Probably it would be best to start with something simple.

'Dad?' said a little Bonny from the garden.

'Hey you,' said Robert, stepping out of the shed. 'You want to help me?'

'Yes please,' said Bonny. 'Can I use a hammer?'

'Not just yet, kid. We need to decide what I'm making first.'

'Make a little house for little people to live in.'

'A dollhouse?'

'No. Not for dolls. For little people.'

'Right. Of course. Do you know any little people who are in the market for a house?'

'Um. No. Not right now.'

'Maybe I shouldn't build a little house till I'm sure of having a buyer at the end.'

'Make a huge giant box.'

'A box?'

'A huge giant box.'

'You might be onto something there, my friend. This calls for research.'

'What's research?'

Robert swung his daughter into piggyback position and headed into the house. 'Research, lass, is finding out about things you don't know. So, if you found a new Thomas train and you didn't know its name, what would you do?'

'Um, I would ask you and you would tell me. Or I would watch the TV until that train was on and see what the other trains called it.'

'Right. And that would be doing research. And the best thing about doing research is that once you've done it you always get to have a snack.'

'I love snacks.'

'Me too. We can have scones.'

'With jam.'

'Correct.'

Robert sat with Bonny at the dining room table, peering at pictures of chests and wooden boxes on his laptop.

'I like that one,' said Bonny, pointing at a large carved chest that seemed to be depicting the sacking of Troy.

'I think that one might be a bit complicated, pal. I was thinking more like this.' Robert pointed at a simple, panelled chest.

'No,' said Bonny. 'It's boring.'

'It's not boring. It's classic. It's simple and elegant.'

'It's boring.'

'Well, I'm the master carpenter in this situation. You're just the apprentice.'

'What's a perentice?'

'It means you have to do what I say. I make all the decisions. And in exchange, I bless you with my wisdom.'

'No.'

'Yes.'

'That's not fair.'

'That's life, champ.'

'No.'

'Tell you what, you can choose what kind of jam we have on our scones.'

'Strawberry. No, raspberry. Um . . . Strawberry.'

'You see. Making decisions is the hard part. Aren't you glad I have to do it instead of you?'

'No.'

'Right. Good.'

Robert spent the rest of the afternoon measuring and sawing, obsessively checking and rechecking the instructions he'd printed out. He felt very manly and proud of himself when he arranged all the pieces into different piles, and to prove it he grabbed Mara's arse when she came out to check on him.

'Look,' he said. 'I am man. I build.'

'Congratulations,' she said. 'You've built some small piles of small wood.'

'You don't have to pretend you're not impressed, woman.'

'Oh, I am. Were it not for our small daughter, playing just outside the door, I'd have you right here, on your doubtless uncomfortable structures.'

'She'll be fine. Come on.'

Mara laughed. Somehow her laugh seemed unsure, as if she could have just as easily cried. She looked relieved. 'I'm too hungry. Cook for me first, then we'll re-evaluate.'

'Ah. First I shall need to hunt the mighty bison. Where be my spear, wench?'

'How lucky I am to have as burly a man as you in my bed.'

'You think I'm burly?'

'And a man.'

'But I'm not in your bed at the moment. But I can be. Just give me a moment, you won't want all this sawdust in the sheets.'

'Dinner!'

Robert patted her on the tummy as he left the shed. 'All right, you. Cool your jets.'

He walked inside, a satisfied smile on his face.

Jake.

Jake faces away from his house, watching the dog over the road. He doesn't like that dog. He's not afraid of it, he just doesn't like it. It is never friendly and happy to see people like Jake's cousins' dog. He always seems to be waiting to see what he can get out of a person.

Jake is thinking about how much he doesn't like the dog when the first flake of snow falls on his arm. He looks up at the sky and a second flake falls on his nose. He turns back to his house and calls for his mum to tell her, to tell her it's snowing. He wants her to come out and stand with him, to stare up at the sky, which is becoming more and more full of little white spots, floating unconcernedly down to earth.

Jake looks at the ground, willing the snow to stay, hoping it won't melt as soon as it hits the ground, but it does, of course. It is barely there a moment before it's lost.

His mother still hasn't come out. If she doesn't come out soon they will be late for the doctor. Jake doesn't care. He doesn't like the doctor, with her sugary voice and sickly perfume. He wonders if she has to have extra-strong perfume because of how much time she has to spend with other people's feet.

The snow that has landed on Jake is melting and dripping down the back of his collar. It makes him shiver but he doesn't want to go inside. He wants to stay and watch. He is mesmerised and still until the ground moves. Of course, it's exactly what would happen if the worlds in snow-globes were real. The houses would fall down. The people in them could never survive.

Jake felt like he could yell in frustration, or punch something. Snowing? Of course it wasn't snowing. It would never have been snowing at that time of year. If it had it would have been some kind of ridiculous record, it would have made the news. But of course, only the disaster made the news; no one had bothered to mention the weather. No one cared.

Jake cared, though. He needed to figure it out. It was such a simple part of it, such a stupid thing to not remember.

Jake's room was messy again, but not with his stuff. There was a light spread of his findings across the floor. A sparse sheet of what people had lost. It was made of books and dolls and bracelets and hats. There were lost sweaters and pens and balls and trophies and Jake knew what had happened to all of them.

He was adding to his collection every day now. Some things he brought home from school. Things that had been left in the Lost and Found room for ages. Some things he stumbled over as he walked around his neighbourhood.

When he found something, he had to come home immediately to find a space for it and chart it on his map. He'd stopped paying attention to whether or not his dad was in the house. It didn't seem to matter. He had too many other things to think about.

Sometimes he would think he was home alone and he'd sit in the kitchen or the lounge and then realise that his dad was not only home, he was in the same room. Jake didn't know sometimes if his dad had come in without him noticing or if he'd been there the entire time.

'Hi Dad,' he said the first time this happened.

His dad took a moment to look at him and when he did, his eyes took a moment to focus, they kept sliding over Jake and back across, as if he wasn't sure where to look.

'Oh,' he said eventually. 'Hi Jake. How are you? How's school?'

'It's good. How's work?'

'Oh. Good.'

'I'm going to go to my room now, Dad.'

'OK, Jake. Sleep well.'

Jake did not tell his dad that it was only four in the afternoon.

Cassie.

CASSIE THOUGHT JASPER WAS TALKING to her, but as he drew closer she realised he was on the phone.

'Are you staying with him tonight?' he was saying. 'Do you want me to come over when I'm finished? It's fine, it's only an extra forty-five minutes. Are you sure? All right. OK. I'll see you tomorrow then. Say hi. You too.'

He glanced at Cassie as he slipped his phone into his pocket. He rubbed his face with his hands and dropped to the floor, sitting with his arms propped on his knees.

'Hi,' he said.

'You look exhausted,' Cassie replied. 'Which, actually, you do quite a lot.'

'Yeah, that'll happen.'

'Sure. Trying job, then, strolling around the airport?'

'Cold, you are, Cass. Well cold. I just have a lot going on at the moment.'

Cassie nodded quietly.

'Exam in the morning, for one thing.'

'Exam? For what?'

'Oh, my degree,' said Jasper. I'm studying physics.'

'Jeepers.'

'Yep. First in my family to go to university.'

'Hey, really? Me too.'

'Huh.'

'Worried about the exam?'

'Mainly worried my girlfriend's going to miss all hers. She's meant to have two tomorrow.'

'Why would she miss them?'

'Her dad. He's not quite himself at the moment.'

'Maybe that's going around.'

'He was amazing, her dad. Genius pianist. Now, he's sort of falling apart.'

Cassie was silent. She'd had no idea Jasper had so much going on. He always seemed so relaxed, as if there was nothing in the world to bother him. Even now, when he was talking about it, there was only the faintest crease in his forehead to show his worry.

'I don't know how you keep track of so many things at once.'

Jasper laughed. 'Everyone does.'

'Do they?' said Cassie. 'I don't think I do. I only have one thing.'

'No you don't.'

'Only Floss.'

'Why, then? What made that happen?'

Cassie thought for a moment. 'She was going to change my life.'

'Yeah? How?'

'I don't know exactly. She just was.'

Floss had told Cassie that she would change her life. 'I'm going to change your life,' she'd said, glibly, casually, as if such a thing were easy and inconsequential. And Cassie had believed her. She'd believed that when Floss returned, her life would properly start. That it would be vibrant, that it would be real. As if everything before had just been practice.

She knew that she could never be exciting on her own.

'Well,' said Jasper. 'That's a bit of a cop out.'

'What?' asked Cassie.

'Sorry,' said Jasper. 'I'm tired. I need to get back to it.'

He stood up and rubbed ineffectively at the grass stain on his elbow.

'Just give me a shout. If you need anything.'

Delia.

'My dear,' said Donald to Delia as he ushered her out of the car and into the house, 'would you like a cup of tea and a slice of chocolate cake before the class starts? I think we've time.'

'Of course I would,' Delia said. 'Of course, I always do.'

She followed him through to the kitchen and sat down just as Mattie flowed in. 'I'm sorry, Delia, it's a giant cock up, obviously, isn't it? It always is.'

'I'm sorry?' said Delia.

'It's all my fault, naturally, I just went and bloody booked two models for tonight.'

'Oh.'

'And, it's fucking horrible, and I'm sorry to be such a fucking pain in the arse, but I asked the other girl first, you see, and then completely forgot about it, and asked you as well. Giant cock up.'

'Oh. It's OK. Um, if Donald doesn't mind driving me home again.'

'Well, my darling one, I actually thought, if you're interested, you could just join the class. For free, obviously, as it's because of my idiocy.'

'Oh, but I don't—'

'Just for fun; you don't need to worry about being assessed if you don't want to be. But please do, it would make me feel so much better about fucking everything up for you.'

175

Delia paused, her heart thumping. She hadn't held a paintbrush in years.

'I don't have any—'

'Nonsense, obviously you'll use anything you want of mine. I mean, not my best, obviously, only I use that, but not the horrible battered things I keep for the dross who insist on forgetting their own all the time either. I'll give you nice brushes. Or pencils. Or whatever. Please do.'

Delia swallowed. 'Um. OK?'

'Marvellous,' said Mattie. 'Now, come up with me, we'll cadge you one of the good spots.'

In the studio a girl, a much younger girl than Delia, was doing stretches in the corner by the screen. Delia wondered suddenly if she should have been doing stretches all this time. It seemed sensible. Mattie dragged her over to the store cupboard and opened one of the drawers inside it.

'Now, since you're not a confident painter you may want to just stick to charcoal.'

Delia bit her lip. She looked over at the easels and back into the drawer of Mattie's middle-quality art supplies, before grabbing a handful of brushes and some acrylic paints.

'Perfect,' said Mattie. 'I thought so.'

As the rest of the class began to trickle in, Delia set herself up beside the window.

The model shed her robe and sauntered into the middle of the room.

'We're going straight into it today,' said Mattie. 'We'll do a half-hour pose, then a few short ones, and another half-hour to finish.'

Delia squeezed a few fat worms of paint onto the plastic box she was using as a palette and began to mix colours. She began painting the model's pensive, downturned face a mossy-brown colour.

It was all still there. The brush felt familiar and comforting, as if she'd painted every day for years.

176

As she worked, Delia began to be less aware of the class around her. Soon she was ignoring even the model as she got sucked into her own painting.

'All right,' called Mattie. 'That's time.'

She came up behind Delia as the model stretched again and prepared for the next set of poses. 'Good work, my girl. Those colours are extraordinary. Although, the point of this class isn't so much to be as fanciful as all that.'

Delia looked again at what she'd painted. The green face gave way to paler shoulders that flowed into arms. Instead of hands, the arms led to a cluster of delicate brown branches, covered over in leaves. Her waist sloped into rough bark on her hips, and grew down into a twisted trunk, spreading its roots into the floor.

Robert.

IN SPITE OF HIS EXCESSIVE caution, it took Robert less than a week to finish the chest. He tried quite hard not to feel smug, but he really did think it was pretty good.

'Look, my daughter,' he said to Bonny, who was sitting on his shoulders. 'Look at what your father has created. From a pile of rubble, I have built Storage.'

'It's boring,' said Bonny.

'Incorrect, dear girl. It is wondrous. It is a thing of beauty and joy. It is my previously latent potential to build such glory that has prevented your mother leaving me all these years.'

'What?'

'Never mind. I am brilliant. That is all you ever need know.'

Mara hugged him a little too fervently when he brought her out to see it.

'It's not that surprising, is it?' Robert said. 'That I managed to construct a thing without losing a digit.'

'It needs varnish.'

'Yes, well, fine. Obviously.'

Robert paused and looked down at her. 'You OK?'

'I'm brilliant. I'm happy you've done this.'

'If I'd known carpentry was all it took, I'd have discovered the shed ages ago. We're talking full minutes here.'

'OK, you,' said Mara. 'Go varnish your chest.'

'I'd rather varnish yours.'
'Please. You can't handle it. And I have work to do.'
'Then leave me, strumpet. Leave me to my impressiveness.'

Mrs Featherby.

'I FIGURED SOMETHING OUT,' Small Girl Bonny called through the plastic barrier. She hadn't come over officially for tea this time, although she had once or twice more since her first visit.

Mrs Featherby looked up from the skirt she was mending. 'Hello, Small Girl Bonny. Do you want to come in?'

'Um, no. It's not a tea day today, is it?'

'It's not a pre-arranged tea day, but that doesn't mean it's not a tea day at all.'

There was a silence from the silhouette. 'I figured something out,' it said again.

'All right. What did you figure out?'

'I figured out that you haven't always been alone all the time.'

'Oh,' said Mrs Featherby. 'How did you figure that out?'

'Your name is Mrs. Mrs is the name you get when you get married. So you had a husband one time, I think.'

'Ah.'

'What was your husband like?'

Mrs Featherby smoothed her hands over the stitches she'd made and began going over them a second time. She was glad Small Girl Bonny had elected to remain on the other side of the plastic.

'His name was David,' she began. 'He was tall and black haired and he had a moustache. He flew planes. We met when we were both in France, although we were from the same part of England. On our honeymoon I taught him how to ride horses, he never

180

had before. After we'd been married four years his plane crashed. And he died.'

There was further silence from beyond the plastic. Then: 'That's a very sad story.'

'Well,' said Mrs Featherby, 'it's not a true one. I was on an assignment, you see, a mission, and I got hurt. My back was damaged and it was going to take a long time to recover. I spent quite a few months in hospital, and when I was well enough to leave, it was still going to be a long time before I was ready to work again, so I came here. I knew that I would be here for longer than I was usually in one place, and I needed a story. When something's happened to you that shouldn't have happened, when someone has died before they should have died, people don't know how to talk to you, so they don't ask questions.'

'So, that is just the story you told to everyone?'

'Actually, I never did. I had it ready, but no one ever asked. You're the first person to hear it, Small Girl Bonny. I hope you enjoyed it.'

The Ring.

ITEM: RING

Place found: School playground, in dirt beside rubbish bin.

The ring belonged to a girl who has still not admitted to herself that it's gone. In spite of the fact that she's moved twice since, she tells herself that it's bound to turn up one day. One morning, when she's not looking for it, there it will be, sitting on the lid of a long-abandoned tub of moisturiser, or in the pocket of a pair of jeans.

In reality, she didn't lose the ring at home, so this can never happen.

It slipped off her finger as she fought her way through the crowds in London Bridge Station at quarter to nine on a Thursday and she didn't notice its absence until hours later. She went to take it off so she could put on some hand cream, and there it was: gone. She decided she must have neglected to put it on after her morning run, and forgot about it for the rest of the day. She remembered two days later and searched at home, but it wasn't there.

The ring had been a gift from a man who later deceived her. It was the one gift she'd had from him, in three years of entanglement, and the one thing she could use to convince herself that he really wanted her, in spite of everything he did. After it was gone, his coldness became more apparent. His failure to show up, his refusal to acknowledge her successes, they were no longer tempered by the one sign of affection the ring had been.

Delia.

DELIA HAD DECIDED SHE WAS going to have to try to find ways of getting around on her own. She'd made it to the supermarket and back by writing out directions in excruciating detail. She hadn't really needed to go, she always had everything delivered anyway, but she invented an excuse just to give herself the challenge. The journey time was half an hour, which she decided was very nearly worth the three hours the directions had taken her to write.

A week later she went to the movies by herself, a journey that involved a bus, so had room for greater error. This too, was a success, thanks to her five pages of notes.

After a month of small steps, she was ready to give the tube another go. She called Anthony.

'I'm having a cider on the South Bank,' she said. 'Come and meet me?'

She was on her second by the time he arrived.

'Where were you trying to go and why didn't you call me?' he asked.

'Here. And I did call you. I called you just now.'

'How did you get here?'

Delia waved her sheaf of paper. 'I wrote it down. All of it. Step one is "Turn left onto street". Two is "Walk past eight houses".'

'That's ridiculous.'

'Well, we're just going to have to face up to the fact that this might be what I need to do from now on.'

'It isn't what you need to do. You can just call me.'

'That's worse. Or at least as bad.'

'Oh.'

'Not because it's you. I mean, kind of because it's you. I just don't want to be some girl who needs her boyfriend to take her wherever she wants to go.'

'Right.'

'I mean, if you were my boyfriend. Are you my boyfriend?'

'I think so.'

'Well then. It hasn't been acceptable to rely on your boyfriend to take you places since you lot all went away to war and we stayed here making factories or whatever. I can do it on my own. It's just harder. Which is OK; there are lots of people who find doing things harder. People who are in wheelchairs, or missing an arm, or really short.'

'But if they had something that took the place of that, they'd probably use it.'

'Thank you, but I do not want you to be my prosthetic arm.'

'How long did that take you to do?'

'I'm not telling you.'

'Ah.'

'It's not because I'm embarrassed about it, it's just that it's my problem.'

'If I'm your boyfriend—'

'I thought we'd just established that you are.'

'Yes, so doesn't that mean that part of my job is to help with your problems?'

'OK, first, being my boyfriend is not a job. Second, yes, but I get to choose when you help and when I do something myself.'

'What if I disagree?'

'You can voice your objections and I will seriously consider them before overruling them.'

'This is ridiculous.'

'You can't be going out for hours every day to help me find my way around. You've an actual job.'

'Yes, but I freelance, I get to do it whenever I want. If I spend the day with you, I can just do my work in the evenings.'

'When you should be spending time with your son.'

'What?'

'Well, you should be talking to Jake. Helping him with his homework, advising him about girls.'

Anthony shook his head slightly, as if to clear it.

'Right,' he said. 'I do see Jake, though. He was in the kitchen this morning, when I had breakfast. I think he was having his breakfast too. I saw him.'

'I should hope so. How is he?'

'Fine. He's fine.'

'I should probably meet him, no? I mean, when you think it's a good time, obviously.'

'Sure. Well, now that I'm down here, what shall we do?'

'Just sit. Let's just sit for a while.'

Robert.

It was a Wednesday so Robert had taken Bonny to the zoo. They'd made the zoo trip once before, but Robert figured there wasn't a limit on how many times a five-year-old girl should be exposed to great animals.

There was a boy looking at them as they watched the giraffes. Robert gave him a small smile and glanced around, looking for the adult or group of similarly-aged children he must belong to.

'Hello,' said the boy.

'Hello,' said Bonny.

'The giraffes are my favourite,' said the boy.

'Giraffes have billions of bones in their necks. My dad knows the actual number. He knows all of the things. Where's your dad?'

'What?'

'Is your dad at the zoo, too? I'm Bonny. Who are you?'

'I'm Jake,' said the boy. 'Did you know there have been giraffes for eight million years? Well, not giraffes exactly, but things like them.'

'Wow,' said Bonny. 'How do you know? Did your dad tell you? My dad tells me all the things.'

'Um, I don't know.'

'Or did your mum? My mum tells me things too, but my dad more because he doesn't have to do working.'

Robert decided he should intervene. 'Are you OK?' he asked the boy. 'Are you here with school?'

186

'Oh, no. I'm fine. I was just looking for something. I should get back.'

Robert was a bit concerned as he watched the boy walk away, but he did seem old enough to navigate the zoo and find his way back to whichever group he was a part of. He and Bonny turned and went off to find the lions.

Cassie.

IT TOOK ONE MONTH, TWO weeks, and six days for the bark to reach Cassie's boobs.

She was never alone now, Jasper checked on her daily and her mum would leave only when Bridie was there.

Sometimes the airport staff – the flight attendants and shop workers – would talk to her, but something in their manner was odd, as if they were trying to talk normally, trying not to show how strange they found her. One of the security guards would always try to linger close by in case anyone needed moving on. In case anyone got too invasive. She knew Jasper had asked them to.

It was only then, when she was more tree than girl, that a letter arrived.

Cass,

I'm sorry.

I do love you. But I'm not coming back yet. Not now.

There were so many words in the first version of this. But they didn't really say anything. I hope you're OK.

I love you. I love you.

See you sometime.

Floss

After another week, when the bark began tickling her armpits, Cassie showed Bridie.

'Well,' said Bridie. 'What do you know?'

'She said "Not now",' said Cassie. 'So maybe that means she's coming back later.'

'She's not coming back.'

'How do you know?'

'All that means is that she has a vague inclination to maybe come back, maybe, one day, for a while, maybe, if nothing else is going on, and she's nowhere better to be, maybe she'll pop over for a bit. Maybe. Probably with a hot girlfriend on her arm. Or even a boyfriend; I wouldn't put it past her.'

Bridie's tone was dark, as if she was determined to be personally offended by Floss's potential future lovers. Cassie didn't say anything. She let Bridie continue, let her vitriol grow until she had repeated herself enough to be aware of it and grow silent.

Floss loved her. She still loved her.

They had been in Floss's tiny flat the first time she'd said it. Floss's vile flatmates had both gone away for the weekend, and the weather was horrible. Cassie and Floss sat watching foreign movies for eight hours straight. They'd been spending almost all their time together – Cassie's other friends had been annoyed – but nothing had really been said or done by either. The credits had been rolling and their drinks had been empty but neither of them made a move to change either. Floss had sat up suddenly and bitten Cassie on the ear.

'What did you do that for?' Cassie had asked.

'Because,' said Floss, 'I love you.'

'Oh.'

'I'm in love with you.'

Cassie had said nothing, just looked. Then she'd sat up too, so both of them were kneeling on the couch, facing each other. She'd leant forward slowly and taken Floss's head in her hands.

Cassie had never kissed anyone before, not properly, not when it really mattered. She didn't know if Floss had, but it seemed likely.

They hadn't left the flat for the rest of the weekend.

'Anyway,' Bridie was saying. 'Now you know she's not coming. So you can concentrate on getting out of here.'

Cassie didn't reply. She wished she hadn't shown her the letter.

Jake.

There were low piles of lost things all over the floor of Jake's room, spreading and merging, so he had to pick his way carefully from the door to his bed. He lay on top of his bed sheets, gazing at his collection of lost things, feeling the weight of their stories.

When he wasn't at home he would look everywhere for new items to add to it. He'd bought more things from the shop. He'd found some in the park, some in the zoo, some at school. When he was home, he was always in his room. He would re-examine the books and shoes and necklaces he'd found, replaying how they'd come to be lost.

He was only half aware of it himself, but he was seeing his dad less and less. Sometimes it was like he was there, properly there, but he was blurred around the edges. Sometimes it was more like he wasn't there at all, but there was a shadow of him, like a sketch someone had drawn before beginning a proper painting.

When Jake was able to focus on him enough, he thought that his dad couldn't quite see him clearly either.

There was the time Jake was sitting on the floor of the living room, reading a book. One of his mother's favourites. The phone had rung and Jake's dad had got up from the chair where Jake hadn't realised he'd been sitting.

'Hello?' he'd said, sounding eager at first.

'Oh. What? Oh, Jake. Right.' He had swallowed and looked

191

around the room before his eyes came to rest on Jake sitting on the floor.

'Right, no, he's fine. He took a day off school? Yes, of course. Of course he was sick. Right. Thank you.'

After he'd hung up he and Jake had looked at each other for a moment before he sat back down. After a couple of minutes, the room was empty to Jake, although he still remembered the phone call.

They were becoming ghosts to each other.

Marcus.

HE SAT COLD IN THE park in the gathering dark. He knew he should be getting home. She would tell him to get home, if she knew where he was. He could catch a cold, she would say. Even though it was still summer, even though the weather was still warm.

He knew he should be getting home.

But home was so empty.

Home wasn't his anymore.

He would walk, he decided. She wouldn't mind if he was walking, probably.

He walked slowly towards his house. There was a woman loitering on the corner, with a cigarette and a wild mane of curly brown hair. She was standing with her eyes closed as she smoked and as he grew closer she gave a shudder and turned unexpectedly, elbowing him in the chest.

'Oh my god,' she said. 'Please don't tell on me.'

'What?'

'Oh. I mean, I'm sorry.'

'Why would I tell on you?'

'I'm smoking. Smoking's bad.'

'Right.'

'I was supposed to have given up. Before I tried for a baby, that was the deal. And I did, I did give up. And then she started school. The baby. She's not a baby anymore, she's a child. A school child.

193

Anyway, I started smoking again. But no one can know. Her father would kill me. With shock and exasperation.'

'He'll probably notice. When you get home.'

'He has no sense of smell. Bit of a freebie, right? I mean, no, I should stop. I will stop. I just really like it. I'm Mara, by the way, do you live around here?'

'Around the corner. Marcus.'

'Oh my god, you're Marcus Weber.'

He stared and nodded.

'I'd heard you were somewhere near here, years ago. Well, not you. I heard Albert Kane was, and you know. I loved him. I thought, when I was younger, I thought I'd maybe be an actress. But I'm terrible at it. But no. Robert, he saw you play once, in his formative years. It stopped him giving up piano. Well, he gave up a year later than he otherwise would have. He was always telling me he'd take me to see you play sometime, but you retired before he got round to it. So that was sad. He said you had the most amazing green piano.'

'I did. I built it myself. With my father. When I was young.'

'You built it? Yourself? That's ridiculous. I didn't think real people did things like that. I thought pianos grew. I didn't really, obviously. I just, never . . . you know.'

'My father was a master carpenter. He made pianos for a living. In Austria.'

'Wow.'

The woman finished her cigarette and stubbed it out on a nearby rubbish bin.

'Do you still have it?' she asked. 'The green piano?'

He didn't answer right away. He looked down the street to a house at the end that was half covered in huge plastic sheets.

'No,' he said. 'It's gone.'

He nodded at the woman and made to walk on.

'Do you give lessons?' she called after him.

He turned back.

194

'Sorry. Of course you don't. Stupid of me. It's just, my daughter, she tries to play with her dad all the time. But he can't teach her, he's forgotten all the important stuff.'

'I—' he paused. He thought.

'Of course you don't, you're a famous pianist, you don't need to. Stupid. Sorry. It was nice meeting you.'

He watched her as she walked away and headed into the house opposite the one covered in plastic. Then he, once again, turned towards his empty house.

Cassie.

THE ARBORIST HAD BEGUN VISITING Cassie every week to check on her progress. Cassie's mother had tried to stop her, but after all, it was a public space.

'What's particularly interesting,' the arborist was saying one day, when the bark had reached Cassie's shoulders and started creeping down her arms, 'is that the bark isn't that of a sapling.'

'What does that mean?' asked Jeremy, Bridie's boyfriend. Bridie, who loved the arborist, had fought with Cassie's mum over who took the shift during which she'd come. Since the reason Cassie's mum wanted to be there was to fight the arborist, Cassie generally weighed in on Bridie's side. Sometimes Bridie would bring along some of their other friends, sometimes she'd come alone. This was the first time her boyfriend had come, although Cassie suspected he'd been begging to for a while.

'He's insultingly eager,' Bridie had said to Cassie, when Cassie had asked how he was a week earlier. 'He keeps bragging about you to people, and then he loses credit when he has to admit he hasn't seen you himself. He wouldn't be coming to be helpful, you know. He'd be rubbernecking.'

'I don't need help.'

'Pfft. If you realised you do need help, you wouldn't need as much help as you need.'

She didn't know what Jerm had said to convince Bridie to let

196

him come, but she was glad. She'd missed him. She'd missed hanging out with the two of them together.

He had latched on to the arborist instantly, finding everything she said and did interesting.

'I don't know really what it means,' the arborist said. 'But it's interesting. I suppose that if the bark was young, it would suggest that a new tree was growing over the young lady.' The arborist had never bothered to learn Cassie's name. 'The age of it probably means that the young lady herself is indeed becoming a tree. Or perhaps the tree she's always been is making itself apparent.'

'Are you saying our Cass has always been a tree?' said Jeremy. 'Blimey, how'd that one get past us all these years?' Bridie thumped him in the chest.

The arborist was stripping bark away from what used to be Cassie's right knee. 'Mind you, the rate of change is indication of the latter theory on its own, anyway.'

'What are the bark samples for?' Jeremy asked.

'I want to see if the fact that this area is completely removed from natural light is having any effect on the health of the tree.'

'I'd say the tree is having a pretty adverse effect on the health of our Cass.'

The arborist appeared unconcerned by Jeremy's point. She carefully deposited the bark she'd collected into ziplock bags and left.

'Holy Christ,' said Jeremy. 'She's amazing.'

'I told you,' said Bridie. 'She's incredible. She actually doesn't care at all.'

'In her defence, she cares rather a lot, just not about Cass here.'

'That is a very strong defence. Thank you for mentioning it.'

'Anytime. Now, Cass, I've come here for a very specific reason.'

'No you haven't,' said Bridie. 'You've come here to provide general emotional support while we all try to think of a way to first, stop Cassie turning into a tree, and second, stop her mooning over her erstwhile strumpet.'

'Right, my lovely, and I have a specific way to do that.'

'Oh god,' Bridie said.

'Right, so,' Jeremy continued. 'You know, Cass, that I have a younger sister.'

'The one that keeps changing her mind about who her boyfriend is?' Cassie asked.

'Yes, her. Well, I think you're the perfect solution.'

'You want me to be the next boyfriend?'

'I just think, she has such terrible taste in boys, right. She'd be much better off as a lesbian.'

'I don't think I'm really up for turning someone gay just at the moment, Jerm.'

'That's not a particularly PC way of talking about this, is it?'

Bridie sighed. 'Jeremy, I'm pretty sure there are only three or four people in the entire world who make less sense than you.'

Cassie laughed. 'Why don't you just try introducing her to some nice boys?'

'Do you think I haven't tried?'

'Yes,' said Cassie. 'I do think that.'

'Well,' said Jeremy, 'you may be right. But that's only because none of the boys I know are anywhere near as nice as you.'

'So get some better friends.'

'Right. Good point. You women folk are always so logical. That's exactly why everyone should always date women and no one should date men.'

'OK,' said Bridie. 'You've convinced me.'

'Excellent. Can you two please make out now?'

Cassie laughed as Bridie and Jeremy continued to bicker. She and Floss had never bickered. They'd not had enough time to develop the habit. They would, Cassie thought. When Floss arrived they would learn to bicker.

Mrs Featherby.

Mrs Featherby was expecting Bonny but when she entered the sitting room the silhouette she found was fully grown.

'Can I help you?' she asked.

'Oh,' said the silhouette. 'Hello. I just wanted to apologise, actually, about Bonny pestering you all the time.'

'You are Bonny's mother?'

'Yes. I'm Mara. I've been meaning to come and introduce myself for a while, but I've been having to work a lot at the moment.'

'How nice to meet you,' said Mrs Featherby. 'I'm Mrs . . . I'm Wendy.'

'We've told Bonny that she shouldn't bother you so much, but she's so certain you like talking to her, and we didn't want to forbid her outright. We don't want to tell her people don't like her company, you know? And Rob said you didn't seem to mind. Not that he'd notice if you did.'

Mrs Featherby paused for a moment before answering. 'It's perfectly all right; she's not doing any harm.'

'Well.' Mara sounded unconvinced. 'Please do let us know if you get tired of it. She's persistent.'

'Naturally I will. Thank you.'

Mrs Featherby waited for a farewell, but Mara didn't move.

'She gets it from me. It's worrying.'

'You mean your persistence is a bad thing?'

Mara paused. 'Oh. I don't really mean anything.'

'You do, I think,' said Mrs Featherby. 'You do mean something.'

'Fine, but I don't *know* what I mean. Yes, I think — it is a bad thing. Or if it's not a bad thing itself it has caused bad things.'

'How exactly has it done that?' asked Mrs Featherby.

'I was persistent about my career, you see, when it looked like I would never get there. Rob slaved away at his job so I could pursue mine and it became a habit for him. Neither of us realised he was unhappy. Now who knows what he's going to do. And if I'd backed off, he could have relaxed years ago, taken some space to figure himself out without it being this fraught thing.'

Mrs Featherby wasn't sure what Mara was talking about, but it seemed rude to ask for clarification. She remained silent and let the young woman continue.

'I can't help but feel,' Mara went on, 'that the reason for everything that's going on with Rob at the moment is my having made the wrong choices.'

'That's a very strongly defined term, dear, "wrong choices", and I'm not sure it's helpful. There are no wrong or right choices, necessarily, just those you make or don't make and the consequences. And by extension, how you deal with the consequences.'

'That's quite seriously philosophical of you.'

'It's simply a less complicated way of looking at things.'

Mrs Featherby listened as the young woman on the other side of the plastic took a deep breath.

'Yes, well,' said Mara. 'Thank you again for how good you've been with Bonny. We'll have you over for dinner one of these days.'

Mrs Featherby pursed her lips. 'Oh not at all. That's not necessary.'

Mara laughed. 'Well, we'll do it anyway. I have to get back to work, I'm afraid. It's been just ace talking to you.'

'Indeed,' said Mrs Featherby.

She watched as the shadow of Mara faded from her wall and sat down to wait for Bonny.

Robert.

ROBERT WAS STANDING, CHISEL IN hand, staring down at the piece of heavy wood on the bench in front of him. It was going to become a low table, but he'd decided to carve narrow grooves into it, close to the edges. He lowered the chisel to the wood.

Robert wasn't entirely sure how long he spent in the shed that afternoon. As soon as the metal touched the wood he felt some kind of concentrated electrical pulse down his arm; he wasn't sure if it was he himself becoming so focused on his task that all his energy was directed to doing it, rather than thinking about it, or if he was completely disengaged. He never consciously decided what he was carving, and it was only once he'd finished that he was able to look clearly at what he'd done.

Curls unfurled themselves over the surface over the wood, spiralling out from the lower right corner, interlocking and over-flowing. Down in the corner was the barely suggested face of a woman.

He stared at it for a few moments before suddenly dashing inside to get Mara.

She looked at it for a moment. 'God that's ugly,' she said. 'I mean, extraordinarily well done, I'm very impressed and all that, but holy hell it's a hideous style of thing.'

'Is it?' said Robert.

'Oh yeah. Not that that's a bad thing; there are loads of people with awful taste.'

'Are you saying I should sell it?'

'Obviously you should. We can't put it in the house; people will think I chose it. Weren't you meaning to sell all this anyway?' She waved vaguely at the stacked chests and stools and jewellery boxes.

'Well, kind of, but I thought you'd think that was stupid.'

'I think you're stupid, does that count?'

Robert looked back down at the spiralling hair.

'Do you really think it's ugly?'

Mara pinched his arse. 'I really do.'

Delia.

'BREAKFAST IS AN ALL RIGHT date, isn't it?' said Anthony.

'You've stopped talking about Jake,' said Delia.

'What? I mean, you don't get candles, but it's still pretty good.'

'Why do you not mention your son anymore?'

'And it sets you up for your day well, doesn't it, making breakfast exciting and special?'

'Anthony.'

'What?'

'How is Jake?'

It was like Anthony couldn't hear her, like any mention of his son was white noise, a conversation happening at someone else's table. Delia didn't know what had happened. She didn't know what to do. Throughout the morning she tried again and again to bring up Jake, but there was no response.

'I have to go,' she said finally. 'There's something I need to do.'

'Do you need me to take you somewhere?'

'No; I have directions home. That's all I need for now.'

'Will you call me to let me know you've got there?'

'Probably not.'

'It's like you want me to come frantically looking for you.'

'I really don't.'

'So just call.'

'I'll think about it.'

Mrs Featherby.

MRS FEATHERBY HAD A RARE and unexpectedly sweet smile on her lips as she sifted flour, but no one was there to see it. She herself wasn't aware of it. She cracked eggs and stirred in chocolate and if you were watching, you'd be sure that she was about to hum.

It was just about that time of day that a small girl could be expected to appear on the other side of the plastic wall. Bonny was always pretty set on not making normal days tea days on the spur of the moment, but if there was a cake, fresh from the oven, there was a chance she might change her mind.

Mrs Featherby poured batter into a cake tin and slid the tin into the oven before walking through to the sitting room. She glanced over at her white plastic wall, but there was no child-sized outline waiting for her. She chewed her lip for a moment and went back to the kitchen to make a pot of tea. When she carried it through, the plastic sheet was still blank.

Mrs Featherby sat with her tea and a book that she did not read for half an hour. She cleared away the tea things, returned to the lounge and still there was no Bonny.

Good, she thought to herself. There was no need to patiently listen to childish ramblings. No need to prudently answer impertinent questions. The afternoon would remain peaceful.

Mrs Featherby took her cake from the oven when it was done. She let it cool. She iced it, placed it in a cake tin and put it on its appropriate shelf in the pantry. She carefully washed her bowls and spoons and tins. She dried them thoroughly and returned them to their drawers and cupboards.

She went back to the sitting room and sat.

Cassie.

FLIGHT ATTENDANT MAEVE DIDN'T REALLY know why she wanted to talk to Cassie that day. She was stressed and tired and still a little afraid she might catch whatever it was that was causing the girl's bizarre and frightening transformation. She decided it was because she couldn't resist taking a moment to sit on the grass, which was at its lushest and most comfortable the metre or two around Cassie.

Flight Attendant Maeve had had a fight with her husband before the trip to Antwerp and back from which she'd just debarked. It was not an original fight; in fact it was almost on its 50th retread.

You should get tested, he'd said, once more, again. We both should get tested, he insisted, so we know what's wrong.

Maeve was offended that he thought there was something wrong, and scared that they'd find that it was her, that she was the problem, that something awful in her was preventing them having a baby.

Flight Attendant Maeve hadn't thought she wanted kids. She'd felt guilty for not wanting them, and more for letting her husband assume she did. It's an odd thing for a woman to say, she thought: no, I don't want to ever push a human out of me. But she didn't. She hadn't wanted any of it. Not the pregnancy, not the birth, not the screaming or feeding or being sick at three in the morning, none of it.

And then one day she had.

At the point of the 47th version of the fertility test argument, they'd been trying for one year, seven months and twenty-two days. They hadn't finished the fight because Flight Attendant Maeve had been running late for work, and she knew it was waiting for her at home. And she knew eventually she'd have to lose it.

Chewing her lip, she approached the terrifying tree-girl.

'Hello,' she said. 'Hello Cassie. It is Cassie, right? Your name? Someone said your name was Cassie.'

'Hi,' Cassie said, and immediately stopped talking.

'Urgh,' Maeve said. 'The weather is so grim.'

There was a pause while Cassie digested this.

'Yes,' she said eventually. 'This is what I hear.'

Maeve cleared her throat. 'Sorry,' she said. 'I just thought, today I just thought, you've been here for ages. And none of us has actually spoken to you. So I thought suddenly "I should speak to her". So. OK. How are you?'

'I'm fine,' said Cassie. 'I'm all right.'

'Good, good. It's so lovely in here now. With the grass, and everything. What . . . I mean, how did it . . . I mean, how did you get here?'

Cassie blinked. 'The tube,' she said.

'Right. And, why?'

'Because of Floss.'

'Oh?' said Maeve. 'Who is Floss? Tell me about her.'

She took off her shoes suddenly, and sat in the grass beside Cassie. Cassie stared and swallowed and eventually started talking.

Floss had sat beside Cassie in a lecture on the French Revolution in the second week of term, it transpired. Floss had asked to borrow a pen, but Cassie was using a laptop and didn't have any with her. Floss had asked to borrow her computer instead.

'How will I take notes?' Cassie asked.

'You don't need to. Haven't you noticed? This guy just reads his slides. Word for word. Then he puts the slides online. To be honest, I'm pretty sure I'm only going to bother coming to this class for another week or so.'

'Really?' Cassie was astonished. 'Can you do that?'

'Yeah, why not?' Floss looked at her closely. 'Although, if you're still planning to come along, I might show up from time to time.'

'Why?'

'You're cute.'

Floss dragged Cassie's laptop over to her. She logged Cassie out of everything and checked her own emails. She showed Cassie pictures of her family, who were mostly in Louisiana, except for a few who were scattered around: a sister in San Francisco, a cousin in Brazil.

Whenever she showed her something new she looked away, waiting for Cassie's reaction before glancing at her to check it was genuine and brushing it away, looking relieved.

Neither of them had gone back to that class.

Flight Attendant Maeve sat with Cassie for about an hour before realising she'd lost the feeling in one leg and had grass stains on her skirt. She said goodbye, and limped away.

When she walked in the front door later that day she called out, 'Fine, whatever, we can do whatever, fine, OK. Fine.' Her husband, Lawyer Josef, said, 'OK.' And they had sex that was almost as fun as the sex they'd had back in the days before they were using it for procreative purposes. Flight Attendant Maeve very nearly orgasmed, and a little spark was lit, which would render her capitulation redundant.

Delia.

Once she was home it took Delia a few moments to find her map and address book and only two and a half hours to write out directions of the detail she needed. Her phone rang several times, but she ignored it.

Travelling always took longer than it should these days because of how often she had to refer to her notes, and the address wasn't close, so it was almost another two hours before she got there.

The front door was yellow.

Delia raised a hand and knocked.

Marcus.

HE WAS ALONE. HE HAD been alone all day. He had been alone all the previous day. She was away. The boy, that Jasper, had taken her away. Jasper was worried, he thought she was stressed and needed a break.

She had called several times and she sounded more stressed by being away, but it was too late now. He was making her worry. He hated making her worry.

He knew the feeling. He had worried about her so easily, so quickly. He had worried about The Woman. He felt she was not to be trusted. He was right.

She told them about the play five months before the baby was due to arrive. I won't work, she had said, I won't think about working, but she had lied.

She sat in their lounge once again and told them of the part she'd accepted. It was perfect, she'd told them, she was perfect for it. It was rare for an actress's pregnancy to coincide with the need for a pregnant actress, she assured them, it was practically a miracle. She was honour bound to accept, she said, and her reward was this part, this wonderful part, this character of all characters.

It was a new play, she said, by an exciting and daring writer. Dealing, she said, with important issues. Issues, she said, that must be addressed.

She would play a middle-class housewife whose husband is murdered while she is pregnant with their second child. Left alone, heartbroken and desperate, she would plummet into a dark hole of prostitution and drug dependency. Her heroin-fuelled suicide would be the most challenging and affecting scene she'd ever performed.

It was necessary, she said, for a role like this to really immerse yourself in the character, to live almost as them. She laughed coyly, coldly, as she assured them that didn't mean she would actually take any of the plethora of drugs the character did. The immersion would be solely mental, she told them, but it would be complete.

He had wanted to forbid her. He had wanted to remind her of her promise. He had wanted to prevent her from ever leaving the house.

He and Albert had fought.

Albert had laughed at her pretensions of total immersion. He had claimed it was a lie actors told themselves because they wanted to believe in the craft of their job. He had claimed they used it to convince themselves they did a harder and more important thing than the designers and operators, and producers and stage crews.

In the end, he had had to let Albert guide him. Albert knew the theatre. They had no legal standing to forbid The Woman anything.

But he had been worried. He had always been worried.

Jake.

THE GIRL AT THE FRONT door looked harried and stressed. She held a sheaf of paper in her hand that had a list on it. The last entry was Jake's house number.

'Are you Jake?' she asked, staring at him as if his answer held the key to her own existence and the very fabric of the universe.

'Yes,' said Jake.

'And Anthony is your father?'

'What?' Jake blinked. The girl had asked a question, but he wasn't sure what it was.

'Shit. Sorry, don't swear. Bugger. I mean, oh dear.'

'Who are you?'

'I'm Delia. I'm a friend of your dad's.'

'What?'

'OK, OK. It's fine. We need to talk.'

'Oh,' said Jake. He wasn't sure who the girl, Delia, was, but she seemed worried. 'Do you want to come in?'

'Right. Sure. OK.'

Jake led her into the house.

'We have tea, I think,' he said and walked into the kitchen.

'Great. Great. Tea is great. OK, but Jake, I need to ask you, when was the last time you saw your father?'

'Um,' said Jake.

'OK. So you haven't seen him in a while?'

'I don't really know.'

'Oh, Christ. This is –' the girl ran her hands over her face, '– fine. It's fine. Let's sit down.'

Jake pulled himself onto the worktop and sat there. His mum had always hated him to do that. The girl, Delia, looked around for a moment then pulled herself onto the worktop opposite him. Jake grinned at her. She smiled back, but she didn't look happy.

'OK,' she said. 'I have to tell you something. I'm a bit worried about you and about your dad.'

'My—'

'Your dad, yes Jake, you have a dad. I really need you to stay with me on this, please. OK? Your dad and I are friends, we've been friends for a while and when we first met, all he talked about was you. All the time; stories from when you were little, and what you were up to in school, all sorts of things. Then, well, something happened with us, and it was probably my fault, and I think it made him unhappy. Actually, that's not true, it definitely didn't make him unhappy, but it changed something. He stopped talking about you, you see. He completely stopped altogether, and I didn't even notice it at first because I'm kind of just totally selfish, I suppose. When I did notice, of course, I asked about you. And the first few times I did, he almost talked about you normally, almost, but I kept forgetting to ask. Because of the selfish thing, you understand. It's not that I don't find you interesting, I just find myself more so. Anyway, as more time passed, when I did remember to ask, he got more and more vague. Your dad, I mean – you still with me on that? And so I got a bit worried and I honestly meant to ask more. But it got to the point that when I did he just didn't respond at all, like he couldn't even hear me. So I was scared and I came here and it was really hard for me to find it, but I did.'

Jake blinked slowly, trying to absorb what Delia was saying. His dad. About his dad. He couldn't concentrate on it. He couldn't remember. Delia was leaning forward and staring at him.

213

He could tell she expected him to say something, but he was empty of words.

'Jake,' she said, suddenly a lot quieter. 'Do you have any photos? Any family photos?'

'Yeah. There are some in the living room.'

Jake slid off the worktop and led Delia through to the living room. He pulled a photo album from the bookshelf and handed it to her. She opened it at random and pulled out a photo. It was Jake on one of his birthdays. His mother was cutting the cake. She'd made him a cake shaped like a raptor and she was cutting off one of its feet.

'Jake,' said Delia. 'Look at him. Look at your dad.'

Jake looked at the man in the photo, standing behind Jake, a hand on his shoulder, looking at the woman as she severed the dinosaur's foot.

'Think about your father.'

And Jake did. He thought about his dad. He remembered him. He hadn't seen him in months. Or had he? He suddenly felt like he'd been seeing his dad all the time, that they'd eaten breakfast together, or, if not together, at least simultaneously, the day before.

'What's happening?' he asked Delia.

'I'm not sure. I think you're losing each other.'

'Oh. Where is my dad at the moment?'

'Probably looking for me. We need to figure out what to do, Jake.'

'What do you mean?'

'We need to figure out how to stop you losing each other.'

Jake looked at Delia, trying to hold on to what she was saying. It was hard and he was tired.

'I've lost things before,' he said. 'People lose things all the time. I've met lots of people who have lost things. It doesn't matter. You still just have to go on with your life.'

'Yes, well, that's very philosophical of you, Jake, but sometimes you really have to do something to stop yourself losing things you don't want to lose. Like those key rings that were around for a while that beeped when you clapped so you didn't lose your keys.'

'But sometimes there's nothing you can do. You said you didn't know what to do.'

'No, but we can figure it out.'

'How do you know we can?'

'Because we have to.'

Jake stared at the girl, Delia. She seemed very nice, but he was having trouble keeping track of what she was talking about. One moment he knew they were talking about his dad, and he knew why, the next she was just a stranger in his house, holding a half drunk cup of tea and a photo album. She looked like she could cry at any moment. Jake didn't want her to cry.

'Do you want to see my collection?' he asked.

'You have a collection?' Delia said. 'What do you collect?'

'I'll show you.'

Jake slipped the photo he was holding into his pocket and walked to the door. He headed to his bedroom, Delia following.

The floor was covered with piles of things. The flotsam and jetsam that were gone from others, spread right to the edges of Jake's small room, so that when he slept, he was surrounded and protected by the loss of others.

'What is all this, Jake?' said Delia.

'They are lost things.'

'What do you mean?'

'They are things people have lost.'

'What people?'

'Loads of people.'

'Where did you get them all?'

'Oh, around. There's a shop round the corner that I bought some from. Sometimes people sell stuff to the shop that someone else just lost. Some things I found myself. Then, I found out that my school has a Lost and Found, and then it turned out that loads of places have a Lost and Found. Cinemas and swimming pools and, just loads of places.'

'Why have you collected them? You don't know whose they are so you can't even return them.'

'I don't want to return them. They're lost. Lost things are lost. But I know whose they are. I can tell.'

'You can tell?'

'I can see them. When I hold things I can see who lost them. I don't know how.'

The girl, Delia, looked like she was about to say something else, when her phone started to ring. Jake tried not to listen to her talk, but she kept looking at him while she did, so it was hard.

'Hello? No, I'm fine. I'm not lost, I wrote directions. It's not stupid. I just have to. And I should be able to sometimes go places without you knowing where I'm going. What if I wanted to surprise you? No, that's not what I'm doing today. Well, actually you might be a little surprised. Um, well, I'm at your house. No, inside. Jake let me in. Jake.'

Jake wondered why Delia was talking to herself. No, her phone had rung; she was talking on the phone. To who, though? She was starting to look like she was going to cry again.

'Yes. I'll wait here for you. I'll make dinner. No, not like that, for the three of us. I need to talk to you both. You and Jake. Just come. OK. See you soon. You too.'

She hung up the phone and looked at Jake. 'Let's make dinner.'

Delia and Jake chatted intermittently as they cooked. Delia felt awkward somehow, as if them talking without having been formally introduced was somehow against the laws of social nicety. Jake was still trying to work out who this person was who seemed so interested in what he was doing.

'Do you miss your mum?' Delia blurted out, for want of something better to say. 'Sorry,' she said immediately. 'That was rude.'

'Oh,' said Jake. 'No one's asked that.'

216

'I'm sorry. I mean, well, I'm sorry.'

'She was really good at cooking. She wrote some recipe books once, but she didn't like other people being able to cook like her so I don't know why she did. Unless maybe the recipes in the books weren't really the same ones she actually made herself. Once, after someone had been taking photos of the food, I tried to eat some chocolate cake, and it didn't taste good like it usually did. It didn't really taste like food at all.'

Delia laughed. 'That's a shame.'

'It's OK. Chocolate cake's not my favourite anyway.'

'What's your favourite?'

'I like banana cake, mainly.'

When Anthony turned up, Delia tried again to explain the situation, this time to them both.

'You're saying I've a son I don't remember?' Anthony said. 'That's just a bit ridiculous, Delia, that's not a thing that could have happened.'

'It doesn't matter,' said Jake. 'It doesn't matter whether he's here. It doesn't matter; I'll be fine.'

'Oh, for fuck's sake,' said Delia. 'You're both here, why can't you just take my word for it and talk to each other like normal humans?'

The evening did not go well. Delia grew more and more frustrated with Anthony's refusal to consider the situation possible. Jake was confused and exhausted.

Nothing had changed.

Robert.

ROBERT AND BONNY WERE DOING numbers when they heard the scream. They were adding apples together and subtracting bananas and they were enjoying themselves until Mara started shrieking outside the door.

'You keep going, Bon,' said Robert. 'I'll just see what's going on.'

'I know what's going on,' said Bonny, looking up at Robert as he reached the door. 'Mum saw what you did.'

'Ah.' Robert girded his loins as he stepped into the hallway.

The moment Robert had realised he was in love with Mara she had been yelling at him. He'd been late to pick her up for a show and they'd not been allowed in. He had taken her to dinner instead, and they'd talked normally; at least, he had thought it was normal. They'd had dessert and then got the tube to Mara's flat. As soon as they were inside, she'd turned to him, her hair suddenly wild with wrath.

'I don't know why you thought you could come home with me.'

'What?' Robert said, genuinely baffled, having all but forgotten how the evening started.

'I was really looking forward to that play and it's sold out and I told you not to be late. And then you insist on dinner, and I have to sit there for two hours not making a scene when all I wanted to do was punch you in your stupid face. Why on earth would you just follow me home? You're not getting sex tonight,

218

which means that I'm not getting sex tonight, which also makes me just the angriest.'

'I'm, um, sorry?' Robert said.

'It wasn't a movie, Rob – although for the record I hate being late to them, too – it was a play. You can't be late to plays; if they do let you in, and I think they were perfectly right not to, the actors can see you. They can see you being late and they probably want to hit you almost as much as I have been wanting to hit you all bloody night.'

Robert stared at her furrowed brow and snarling mouth and the words 'I love you' just said themselves.

Saying I love you is quite a good way to get out of a fight when you've not said it before. Robert didn't think it would work in this case.

'Hello, my love,' he said to Mara's back.

'What,' she said. 'What have you done? What is this? What have you done to the bannister?'

What Robert had done to the bannister was strip the paint from it and carve vines all over it.

'What did I tell you,' Mara went on, 'about your fuck-ugly carving?'

'. . .' was Robert's reply.

'If people see this, they will think I had someone in to do it. They'll think it's here on purpose. This is not how I want my house to look. This is not how I want people to think I want my house to look.'

'OK, I know. I know you hate it. I know it's awful. It just happened. I looked at it, thought, ooh that's carvable, and the next thing I knew I was carving it, OK?'

Mara stared at him as if he was crazy. Which was fair, all things considered.

'Are you saying you are liable to carve any wood that happens to be lying around this house into hideousness, even if it's attached?'

'I can't guarantee that that's not the case.'

'I really didn't know that's what I was getting into with this thing. You never said this was going to happen.'

'Yes. I didn't know, of course, but fine.'

Mara ran her hand over the newly ornate bannister. 'Well, eventually we're going to have to move. We're going to have to move somewhere with nothing wood about it.'

Robert took her hands and rested his chin on her head.

'I am quite seriously in love with you. You are probably the most good of all the good things. And you are a fine piece of arse.'

'Christ, boy. There's no need to go overboard on the complimenting me just because I'm being all understanding.'

'You're right. I'll just drag you upstairs and have my way with you instead.'

The Perfume Bottle.

ITEM: PERFUME BOTTLE

Place found: second-hand shop.

The perfume in the bottle wasn't that special. The woman was young and broke and bought the cheapest she could find, more because she liked to have the bottle full than because she was particularly worried about her own scent.

The bottle had been a gift from her best friend when they were both twelve and reading books in which the heroines had dressing tables. It was the sort of bottle that belonged on a dressing table: cut glass with a green-tasselled atomiser.

The young woman didn't lose the bottle. She would never have lost the bottle. The bottle was in her suitcase. She lost the suitcase. It was large and orange and should have been difficult to lose, but she lost it. She sat down in a quiet square for half an hour with a coffee and a book, and when she left, she walked away without it.

The suitcase stood where it was for a few hours until someone came along to clean the square. He dragged it to the nearest skip and left it beside it. The suitcase was on the heavy side and he had a bad back.

It didn't move from the skip until five the next morning, when a middle-aged woman, unable to sleep, took an early morning walk. She removed all the items from inside it, tossing them carelessly aside, and took it home. She'd been meaning to get a new suitcase.

The bottle rolled under a bush, where it sat for three days.

Mrs Featherby.

WHEN THE PHONE RANG, MRS Featherby answered it in what some may have considered an unnecessarily short tone of voice. She'd been sitting alone with a cup of tea, unmolested for the fourth afternoon in a row. There had been no giggling from Bonny, no apologies from her father, no visits for tea.

Mrs Featherby had been restored to her solitary existence, and now her peace was interrupted by the telephone.

'Hiya Mrs F,' said Bruno on the other end of the line. 'How's it going over there?'

Mrs Featherby closed her eyes briefly before answering. 'Fine, thank you. I'm fine. And yourself?'

'Oh, just tops, Mrs F, just tops. Look, the chap with the bricks has come through, he's got them all ready to go.'

'Oh.' For a moment Mrs Featherby didn't know how to respond. She almost felt unsettled, almost reluctant, although this was just the call she'd been waiting for all these weeks. Before she could rouse herself to speak, Bruno went on.

'The other good news is I've Thursday and Friday free, right, so, assuming the bricks arrive tomorrow, which he's assured me they will, we can crack right on. Have you all snug, like, in no time.'

'Well,' said Mrs Featherby. 'That's excellent. Thank you so much.'

'Thought you'd be pleased. Stop those pesky conversations you hate so much.'

'Indeed.'

'Right so, the bricks'll arrive tomorrow, they've said before midday. You don't need to worry, they'll just pop their heads in to let you know they're there, and leave them in the front garden, bit of tarp, all sorted.'

'Splendid.'

'And then I'll be round the day after to start slapping them all together for you, you know. In wall form.'

'That would be most satisfactory.'

'Of course it will. Well, I'll be off then, see you Thursday, Mrs F.'

Mrs Featherby stood silently by the phone for a few minutes. She walked through to the sitting room to retrieve her now-cold tea. She gazed at her white wall. Soon it would be gone. Things would be back to normal. She would be protected from the world. Alone, as she preferred to be.

That was what she wanted, she reminded herself. That was what she'd always wanted. To be left alone.

Cassie.

A BOY CAME UP TO Cassie one day, when the bark was halfway up her neck. He'd been watching her for a while, but not in a way she minded. It was as if he was just trying to figure her out. He didn't assume any kind of ownership, as was so often the way with those who gaped and pointed. He just looked. He looked curious.

'Hello,' Cassie said, when he was close to her. 'I'm Cassie.'

'Hello,' said the boy. 'I'm Jake. Why are you turning into a tree?'

'I don't really know. Maybe it's because I don't want to not turn into a tree enough to be able to stop.'

'Oh. OK. I don't think being a tree is a very good thing.'

'Why not?'

'Because you will get pooped on by birds and peed on by dogs and people will climb you and one day someone will cut you down and make a fire. And you won't be able to stop them. Because trees don't have opposable thumbs. Or any kind of thumb. They're pretty useless in a fight.'

'I think that to not want to be a tree you have to have something that stops you from wanting to be a tree.'

'Like what?'

'Like what I had. Before I lost it.'

'What did you have?'

'Oh, just a person. I don't have her anymore.'

'Your mum?'

'No. Not my mum.'

'Oh. So you still have your mum?'

'Yeah. I lost someone else. And losing people changes you, I guess.'

'That's not true.'

'What?' said Cassie, surprised.

'When you lose something you just lose that thing. That's all that's different. You don't have to be different just because of it.'

'How do you know? What have you ever lost?'

The boy stared at her for a moment. 'Everything,' he said.

Cassie stared back at the boy. 'Who are you here to meet?' she asked.

'I'm not here to meet anyone. I'm just looking for some things. I'm looking for somethings.'

Cassie tried to think of something else to say.

'Bye,' said the boy. 'I hope you get better.'

'I'm not sick.'

The boy looked at her and walked away.

Delia.

DELIA WAS EXHAUSTED. SHE'D SLEPT badly, thanks in part to her now constant worry about Anthony and Jake, and in part to one of her absurdly young neighbours rowdily kicking the other twenty-one-year-old's boy out of the house at three in the morning. The cries of 'She doesn't want you here, why did you even come over, you giant jerk face!' went right into Delia's brain like a needle and lodged there.

She'd walked to the park, carrying what had become her usual sheaf of directions, spread out her jacket and sat on it with a sketch pad. She'd bought it two weeks earlier and left it sitting on her shelf ever since. In the past she would have rushed back to get breakfast ready for her mother, but she knew now that her mother would relish her absence as an opportunity to do things for herself. They were learning a comparative independence from one another.

Delia spent half an hour trying to decide to draw something.

She drew a circle.

She traced over it again.

She drew round and round the same circle until the charcoal was thick and solid and glinting.

After twenty-four minutes she left the park.

'Morning Dee,' her mother trilled as she walked in the front door. Her mother had started trilling. Delia hadn't realised things had gone that far. Delia grinned as she hung her bag on a hook

226

on the wall, but stopped when the hook fell out of the wall and her bag crashed to the floor.

'Morning Mum,' Delia said as she walked through to the kitchen.

'Guess what I did?'

'What?'

'I made you breakfast.'

'You didn't have to do that.'

'Guess what I made you?'

'What?'

'Poached eggs! I made poached eggs.'

'You didn't.'

'I did. I was a bit worried I'd burn the house down, but I wanted to try, and the stove top's not that hard to reach. And I'd got this special poaching set that's quite low and easy to use and I didn't tell you about it because I wanted to surprise you and aren't you surprised?'

'This is amazing, Mum. You're a rock star.'

'You know, I really think I am. We should go out today, you and I. Do you have work to get done? We could go to a matinee.'

'Really?'

'Would you like to? And let's get tea out somewhere. Let's put on nice dresses and do tea and a matinee.'

Delia grinned again and began to make coffee.

Marcus.

HE WALKED SLOWLY THROUGH THE park with his girl, her arm through his. She had come to his house to study because she could concentrate better at his house. She had told the boy, told that Jasper, not to call her today. She was working and spending time with her father and couldn't be distracted.

Her study did not seem that important, though. She'd sat with a cup of tea and a book for a while and when he'd asked her about it, she'd said that it was required reading. He did not think she was studying literature, but he didn't want to ask. He didn't want her to know he understood why she wanted to be always around.

She had said she needed a break after an hour. She had said she needed to get outside for a while. She had said he needed to as well.

And so they walked through the park.

He saw mothers playing with their babies. He saw pregnant women. He wondered if it had been strange for her growing up without a mother. She had known about The Woman ever since she'd been old enough to ask, and had never expressed any inclination to find her. She'd always seemed happy.

They had been two months away from having her when he and Albert had gone to see The Woman's opening night. He had been prepared to be in excruciating pain all evening, worried about how the extremes of emotion through which The Woman was putting herself would affect the child within. He needn't have been concerned.

Although her face contorted itself beyond recognition, changing expression with a speed and dexterity that astounded him, that was as far as the emotion went. It barely made it to her collarbone and had no chance at all of getting to her womb. The baby was safe.

Albert had been right. Of course he had.

Albert had been right about everything.

Mrs Featherby.

THE BRICK MEN INSERTED THEMSELVES in Mrs Featherby's consciousness at one thirty-seven in the afternoon. She hadn't been expecting them to be punctual, but all the same, she had to fight the urge to explain to them what the phrase 'before midday' meant.

They were quick and brutal in their assault on her front garden. They deposited their load callously and efficiently, leaving in their wake a crushed and ruined reminder of what had been a well-crafted bower. Mrs Featherby gave them tea and watched silently as they drank it.

After they left, she gazed into the remaining mess for a while, barely aware of the passage of time. It wasn't until there were school children walking past her, on their way home, that she stirred herself with a jolt, realising suddenly what she had been doing.

She walked through to the kitchen and took the kettle from its stand. She stood by the sink, staring at the tap for several minutes. Finally, she crossed to the phone.

Her first attempt went to voicemail, but on her second try Bruno answered immediately.

'Hiya Mrs F,' he said. 'Problem is there? With the bricks?'

'Not at all,' said Mrs Featherby. 'They've arrived, and they seem fine.'

'Excellent, excellent. Well I'll be over by seven tomorrow, then, if that's OK for you, to start work.'

'Right.'

'Obviously it's going to be a bit noisy and chaotic, but we'll try to have it over with as soon as possible for you.'

Mrs Featherby didn't reply.

'You all right with that, Mrs F?' said Bruno.

Mrs Featherby couldn't see the plastic sheet from where she stood by the phone, but the draughts that had been inescapable since its advent were dancing around her ankles. She reminded herself that this would be getting her back to normal, not changing her.

Once again, people would be barred from her by bricks and mortar. There would be no more causeless intrusions. No overheard whisperings, no photos. No childish chatter.

'Mrs F?'

'Actually, do you know, if it's not too much trouble, I'd very much like to put it off. It's just I, well, I think I have a migraine coming on, I get them from time to time, and if I'm right I won't be able to handle the noise tomorrow.'

'Oh, that doesn't sound good at all, Mrs F. You OK?'

'I shall be, thank you. They can sometimes last a couple of days, you see.'

'Right, right. Never had migraines, but my sister-in-law gets them all the time.'

'They are . . .' Mrs Featherby paused for a moment, trying to think of a word to describe an affliction from which she'd never suffered. 'Unpleasant,' she concluded.

'That's what I hear. Well, I've no problem delaying for you. Thing is, though, I'm booked solid for the next two and a half weeks. I won't be able to fit you in till then.'

'I understand that completely. If you could just come back as soon as you're able, that would be perfectly fine.'

'Okey doke, well, if you're sure. Hope you feel better soon.'

Mrs Featherby walked through to the sitting room. There had been no Bonny. Mrs Featherby sighed. She carried on to the kitchen and began sifting flour.

Robert.

ROBERT WAS SITTING IN A deck chair watching Mara and Bonny build a sandcastle. The sun was beating down on him in a way that would normally put him to sleep, but despite his stillness he was agitated.

He was supposed to be relaxing, the point was to relax, but he was struggling. He couldn't rid himself of the feeling that he should be doing something, that he should be active in his own interests; he couldn't convince himself to calm down.

He watched as Bonny smoothed the sides of her castle before getting up and jumping on it.

Mara's father came and sat on the sand beside Robert and handed him a beer.

'Hell, she's getting tall, that girl,' he said.

'Yep,' said Robert. 'That'll happen.'

They sat in silence for a few minutes before the older man spoke again.

'I'm glad you made it over. It's been too long.'

Robert cleared his throat uncomfortably. Mara's father had moved to this small part of the Portuguese coast shortly after Bonny was born and they'd only ever managed two visits.

'Things always seemed to come up, Geoff. We tried. I always seemed to get so tied up at work.'

'You did.'

Bonny had lain down flat on her back and was forcefully directing Mara to cover her with sand.

'So what do you think you'll do now?' Geoff asked.

Robert looked away and took a sip of his beer.

Geoff continued talking before he could answer.

'It's odd, the way jobs work nowadays. Not how they used to. Everyone seems so sure that you're supposed to know what you want to do, that it's important to find just the right job, and that you have to figure it out early. I'm not so sure that's how it works. Seems to me it's much less complicated to just do whatever you want when you want to do it, for as long as that'll work for you.'

'That's not always practical, is the problem, I suppose.'

'Well, that's true. That is true. I don't have an answer for that.'

Robert let his head fall back against his deck chair and closed his eyes. There was something he had to figure out. There was something he was missing.

He was still sitting there, still but not relaxed, when Mara came up and kissed him. He opened his eyes.

'Your daughter's become a mermaid,' Mara said. 'It's very important you come and see.'

Jake.

JAKE WAS CONCENTRATING. HE WAS drinking milk and concentrating as hard as he could. He was sitting cross-legged in the armchair in the office. The office he almost remembered having been in before.

There was no one else in the room.

Jake focused.

There was no one. Was there? Was there no one else? Maybe there was someone at the big slanted desk. Maybe there was a pencil moving over its surface. Maybe the ruler kept changing position. Maybe there was a voice muttering to itself.

Jake thought that he could just give up. Just let go. But the girl, Delia, had been so nice and so sure and so likely to cry.

He decided to try talking to the room's absence of person. He didn't know what he was supposed to say, but he thought that if he just started saying something, the something he said would carry him along to the next thing.

'I don't really like pizza anymore,' he started. 'I don't know when I stopped liking it, but I did and now I don't think I'll be able to start again.'

Jake talked on and on until he was hungry. He didn't remember much of what he said, but he was almost sure most of it had been true. Sometimes he'd come across something that he really wanted heard and he'd leant forward in his chair and at those times he could swear there had been someone standing in the room. A

234

figure would flash off and on like they were standing on a platform behind a train that was travelling quickly past them. Then he'd find himself with nothing to say and sure there was no one in the room to hear him.

Jake went to the kitchen and got out a loaf of bread. He made himself a sandwich and poured a glass of juice. He carried them back to the office. He stood in the door for a moment, undecided, then he crossed the room and put the plate and glass on the small table beside the desk. He went back to the kitchen and made another sandwich. He turned to go back to the office with it, but changed his mind and stood eating in the kitchen instead.

He sipped his juice slowly and picked up the leftover crumbs with his finger. He ran a full sink of water to wash his few dishes. He wiped the bench. He chewed his lip and then decided he needed to go to the toilet. He washed his hands for twenty seconds. He dried them thoroughly.

He took a deep breath and went back to the office. The plate and glass were empty.

Mrs Featherby.

IT WAS THE FIRST TRULY cold night of the season. The air was bitter. Mrs Featherby lay wakeful and shivering. She was regretting putting off Bruno. She'd been foolish and impulsive and for no reason.

It had been ridiculous of her to feel that she was used to her situation. She had never been used to it. The noise of the plastic, the constant draughts, the cold, the interruptions, all of them had been a drain. That was why she was exhausted now. That was why she felt bleak and alone.

She thought of the small child who'd pestered her so constantly. She had been foolish, she thought, a sentimental old woman, to think that would continue. That a five-year-old girl would continue to find her interesting. She wasn't interesting, she knew that.

It was a relief that she'd not come back, Mrs Featherby told herself, and there was no reason, there had been no reason to delay putting up the wall.

It was her own fault she was so cold. Her own fault for making herself so vulnerable.

Cassie.

CASSIE WAS ALONE FOR ONCE. She wasn't sure how it could have happened. If anyone had known she was alone, there would have been a panicked race to get to her.

She was still not sure what the point of all this attentiveness was. She didn't know if people were worried she'd get lonely, or if they just wanted to make sure someone was remembering her existence. Or maybe they just wanted there to be a witness to her final transformation. Her final moments.

Cassie watched as a small family came through the gates. The father was giving a piggyback ride to the little girl as the mother pushed a trolley with their things. The girl seemed to be peppering her father with questions. After a few minutes she noticed Cassie.

Cassie looked away. When she looked back, the father had put the little girl down.

The little girl came and stood in front of Cassie.

'Hello,' she said. 'My name is Bonny and what is yours please?'

'Hello,' said Cassie. 'I'm Cassie.'

'I asked my dad why you were a tree and he said he didn't know and I should ask you, but it would be rude if I didn't know you. But now we know each other and can I please ask if you are really part of a tree or if you are just pretending?'

Cassie looked down at the small girl for a moment.

'Um, I'm not,' she paused. 'I'm not really sure.'

'Oh,' said the girl.

Cassie looked back over at the girl's parents. Now that he wasn't talking to his daughter, the man looked pale and strained. The animation that had filled his face had bled away. The woman was looking at him. When he noticed her gaze, she rubbed his arm briefly before pressing on with the trolley.

'All right, scamp,' the man said, approaching Cassie and the small girl. 'You've probably pestered the young lady enough.'

He picked Bonny up again and swung her onto his back.

'Sorry about this, miss,' he said to Cassie. 'I'll get her out of your way.'

'She's OK,' said Cassie. 'She's fine.'

The man looked at Cassie for a moment. 'Are you all right?' he asked.

Cassie felt suddenly breathless and sick. She swallowed a couple of times. 'I'm fine,' she said finally. 'I'm OK.'

He looked like he was about to say something more, which Cassie suddenly didn't think she could stand. She turned to the young girl.

'Where are you coming back from, Bonny?' she asked.

'My granddad's house,' said the girl. 'My mum made us go for a holiday. I built five sandcastles and became a mermaid.'

'Wow,' said Cassie. 'I haven't built a sandcastle in years.'

'I'm really good at it. My mum is not very good, but I help her, so it's OK. You are very beautiful. You are a very beautiful tree girl. I wish I was a tree girl.'

'You would make an awful tree girl,' said the girl's father. 'You're always running around and rolling over. Trees have to stay standing in the same place.'

'Oh, OK,' said the girl. 'Maybe I will be another type of girl. Maybe I will be a puppy girl.'

'Let's hope not. Cleaning up after you is enough of a struggle already.'

'Besides,' said Cassie, 'you're already a beautiful normal girl. You don't want to be a puppy girl as well.'

'There are lots of beautiful normal girls. But I am going to be a spy so maybe it's better to look like a normal girl.'

Cassie laughed.

'It's not funny,' said the girl. 'Being a spy is serious and dangerous and you have adventures and made-up husbands and you get sad.'

'Oh,' said Cassie. 'Why do you want to be one then?'

'Because.'

'Right,' said Cassie.

She watched as the small family walked away. She was still gazing in the direction they'd gone in when Bridie arrived.

'Where the hell is your mother?' she asked immediately. 'Why are you alone?'

'I don't know, Bri, but it's fine.'

'No, it's not.' Bridie was unusually shrill.

'Jesus, calm it down,' said Cassie. 'You're as bad as she is.'

'It's just, you shouldn't be alone, you know?'

'No. Why not?'

'Because. What if something happens?'

'It is already happening, someone being here or not isn't going to change that.'

'I know, that's my point.'

Cassie felt a spark of irritation. 'What, are you afraid of the transformation completing itself unwitnessed? You want someone here to take pictures?'

Bridie burst into tears. She looked as if she wanted to run off. Cassie knew she wouldn't: that would mean leaving Cassie alone again. She watched Bridie force herself to stay and they both fell silent.

Cassie chewed her lip and tried not to apologise. She tried to still feel angry.

239

Marcus.

HE WAS GOING OUT TO the theatre. Not Albert's theatre – Albert's theatre had faded and crumbled not long after Albert had faded and crumbled. His girl had thought an evening out might be good for him, so her and her boy, her Jasper, had picked a play to see.

He was finding it harder to leave the house. He'd got lost once or twice, and several times left the house without his house keys. He'd had to wait in the garden until she'd come over to check on him. She was coming over to check on him a lot these days. He knew he was worrying her, and the knowledge of that made him so tired and guilty.

She'd bought him a few new CDs of his favourite composers, but he didn't listen to them that often. It was too much like always hearing strangers talking and never getting to say anything himself. He didn't know how to explain this to her, so he pretended that he liked them and felt embarrassed whenever she turned up earlier than he was expecting to find the house silent.

She always had excuses for coming round. She wanted to find a book she'd left here. She'd found an unusual tea she wanted him to try. She'd been shopping nearby. Sometimes the boy, her boy, was with her. He was nice and energetic, but baffling. He felt so young.

He'd always known really he was too old to be a father. Too old to be a good father. He hadn't expected to be the only one left for her. Albert had been fourteen years younger than him, so, although they were both a lot older than most new parents, it hadn't seemed so outlandish. And when Albert had died, he'd still felt, not young, but of a normal age. Now, suddenly, so suddenly, he was old and failing.

There weren't many people at the theatre when they got there. They'd wanted to be in plenty of time so it wouldn't be stressful for him. They'd wanted to be able to take it slowly. That's what they'd decided he needed to be able to do.

They found a small table in the bar and Jasper got them some drinks. They sat together.

He'd been staring at it for a while before he realised that there was a piano in one corner of the bar. It was closed and had a sign sitting on top of it. Probably warning people not to touch it.

He wondered if it would be the same, this piano. If it would be as hostile as his had become. He would have lower expectations; after all, he would know it wasn't his, or partially his.

His girl, his Katharine, was busy telling them what she'd heard about the play they were seeing. He didn't know if she'd realised he hadn't been listening. He suspected that if she had, she would just have tried to talk harder. He stood.

'Dad,' she said. 'Dad, where are you going? Do you need help?'

He neither turned nor answered. He moved across the room. He didn't look back until he'd reached the piano, sitting alone with its 'please do not touch' sign. As he sat down, he could see that she had tried to follow him and that the boy had stopped her. His restraining hand was still on her arm and she still looked tempted to push the boy aside and go after him. After her one remaining father.

As he raised the lid of the piano, one of the bar staff, a young girl, noticed him there and started towards him. He raised a hand towards her and she stopped walking.

He flexed his fingers. Some Schumann to start.

There were more people around now. All the tables were full and a handful of people were standing. He noticed them start to

241

look, he noticed them begin to listen, and then he stopped noticing much at all.

After the Schumann, he improvised for a while with some jazz. Then he played some Debussy, which he professed not to like but was always soothed by.

He didn't know how long he played for. He kept going until she was standing behind him, with her hands on his shoulders.

'Dad,' she whispered. 'We have to go in now. The play'll be starting in a minute.'

The play was short and odd and funny. He forced himself to pay attention in the way he would have if Albert had been there to talk it over with afterwards. It was the sort of thing Albert would have liked, he thought. Albert would have understood it better than he did.

His daughter and her lover drove him home and came in for tea. She made him sit in the lounge while she and her Jasper got it ready and brought it through. When she handed him his tea cup he found it impossible to grip. His fingers wouldn't close over the handle and he had to hold it with both hands. He put it down quickly on the low table beside his chair and looked at his hands. They were swollen and red. He didn't recognise them.

Delia.

THE DOOR OPENED BEFORE DELIA had even knocked on it. Jake stood there. He looked pale.

'I've been waiting for you. Waiting for ages. He ate my sandwich, I think. I can't quite remember anymore, that's why I wanted you to come earlier. I wish you'd been here straight away.'

Delia felt a flush of guilt. Had Jake called her asking her to come over? No, he definitely hadn't. She hadn't given him her number. Probably she should. Almost definitely she should.

'I'm sorry, Jake,' she said. 'I didn't know you'd want me to come over again. I was worried, actually. I thought that when I got here you'd want me to leave. What happened?'

'I made a sandwich, I think, and I put it in the office, in his office, I think, and I went away and I think I made another sandwich and ate it, and I think that when I went back to the office, the one I'd put there had been eaten. I think.'

'OK,' said Delia. 'That's good. That's really good.'

'If it happened,' said Jake.

'Which we think it did.'

'I think so.'

'Is he here?'

'Um,' said Jake.

'Oh. You can't tell?'

'Well, I think he was here and I'm not sure that he's left.'

'That's good enough for me.'

Delia walked into the house calling for Anthony, Jake walking behind her. She walked into the office. Anthony was standing at his drafting board. An empty plate was on the table beside him. A used glass was on one of the bookshelves. Delia caught Jake's eye and he gave her a thumbs up.

'Hi,' said Delia, giving Jake a nervous wink. 'Oh, did you just eat? I thought we'd have dinner.'

'What?' said Anthony, turning around. 'Oh, hi. Sorry, I didn't know you'd arrived. How did you get in?'

'Wow. You get really distracted when you work, don't you.'

Anthony ran a hand through his hair, which was already standing around his head like a dark halo. 'What? Oh. Sorry.'

'Should I leave you alone for a bit to finish?'

'Um,' Anthony looked vaguely around him. 'No. No, I think I'm finished for now. Are we having dinner?'

'I thought so, but did you just eat?' Delia pointed at the empty plate.

'Oh. No. I don't think so. That was hours ago.'

'What did you have?'

'Just a sandwich.'

'Great. Nice?'

'Yeah. It had something weird in it. I don't know what it was.'

'Coriander,' said Jake. Delia stared at him for a moment, before turning back to his father.

'But didn't you make it? Don't you know what went in it?'

'Of course I did. Who else would have made it? Do you want to cook tonight or shall I? Actually, me cooking is not a good idea. Shall we get something in? There's a good Thai place near here.'

Anthony walked out of the room, still rubbing his outraged hair.

'How did you know about the coriander?' asked Delia. 'Did you hear him say that about there being something weird?'

Jake blinked. 'Yeah. Yeah, I heard everything he said about the sandwich.'

'OK. OK, OK, that's good. What's something else you've done recently? Could you get some pictures you've taken?'

'I'm not supposed to bring things like that to the table.'

'I think we should make an exception this time.'

Delia walked to the kitchen while Jake ran upstairs. Anthony was just hanging up the phone.

'I wasn't sure what you'd want so I just got what I wanted,' he said, grabbing her.

'You could have come and asked,' Delia replied when she had a moment free.

'I like having you in my house,' said Anthony. 'You make my house feel good.'

'Mmm,' said Delia. 'I like being here. And I like Jake. I hope you ordered enough food for him.'

Anthony let her go and grabbed two plates out of the cupboard. Delia rolled her eyes and got out a third.

Mrs Featherby.

MRS FEATHERBY WAS DOZING IN the chair that was by the window that used to exist. She was not in favour of dozing, and she hadn't meant to let it happen, but sometimes we are not altogether in control of such things.

In her hand was a letter on crisp, cream-coloured paper. At the top of the paper was an insignia Mrs Featherby hadn't seen for years. The letter started with the phrase 'It's come to our attention that you are now sufficiently recovered to . . .'; its contents were all the kinds of things she was used to, or had been, long ago: a time, a place, a list of names, an exchange of phrases.

The letter had sent her into a stream of worry and memory, which had in turn lead to a confusion of dreams.

When she woke she was confused for a moment. Her house felt alien and cold, not just because of the plastic, but somehow in a deeper, more real way. She was unnerved, and Mrs Featherby did not like being unnerved.

A voice called out from the other side of the plastic, causing Mrs Featherby to start for the second time.

'Hello,' said the voice, and Mrs Featherby sighed and smiled.

'Hello Small Girl Bonny,' she said. 'How nice to see you.'

Cassie.

THE BARK WAS COVERING CASSIE's lips, and people were finding it hard to talk to her. It's always hard to talk to someone who can't reply. They talked at her, but it always felt as if they were trying to avoid a response rather than encourage one. The people who knew her best had almost stopped talking altogether.

Maeve came to show Cassie terrifying and hilarious facts from her pile of pregnancy books. She never said so, but she wholeheartedly believed Cassie was the reason she'd finally managed to get pregnant. Which meant she was responsible for the jokes and laughs over choosing baby names, the excited shopping for cots and pushchairs, and the general lifting of the cloud Maeve had been living under for so long. Maeve was one of the many who, despite the evidence, didn't truly believe that Cassie's transformation would ever be complete. She couldn't imagine it happening, even though it was, and right in front of her eyes.

Cassie had made another woman in the airport happy, without ever knowing about it. A young deaf girl had heard about the strange situation in Terminal Two of Heathrow Airport and been desperate to see it. A young deaf girl who'd been raised on superstition and wanted to believe in magic. Cherry's daughter came to see the tree-girl at the airport. She stood near her for ten minutes, too shy to approach her and that evening her life changed.

Cherry had made her daughter a late-night hot chocolate before bed. They'd been sitting together quietly when suddenly something had changed. Cherry's daughter looked up, her brow furrowed. She shook her head briefly, as if there was water in her ears, and concentrated. She walked over to the window and looked out into the street.

It was late at night and the street was quiet, but every so often a car would drive past, and for the first time ever, Cherry's daughter could hear them.

Cassie didn't notice that Cherry had stopped glaring at her, and if she had, she wouldn't have thought to ask why.

Her mum would fuss over her, brush her hair, shoo away the curious, but she would rarely say a word. She would avoid looking Cassie in the eye. It was only now that Cassie noticed that she was looking older. It was only now she noticed her mum's ill-fitting clothes, her clammy-looking skin, her broken hair.

Jasper still checked on her frequently, but he was also looking sad more often than usual.

Bridie was quieter than she had ever been. She'd sit in her row of seats, which would now be forever stuck in its inconvenient position, diagonally cutting across the thoroughfare, and read, or write letters. No one else was coming.

Cassie had started to wonder what they'd do once she was all tree. Would they come and visit her? Would they leave flowers, as if the tree was her gravestone? Would the airport let her stay here? Would they try to have her removed?

It occurred to her that she'd picked a pretty average place to become a tree. Surely there was a glade or a grassy knoll somewhere that was short of a tree. But of course, it was too late now. And she supposed that few trees really got to choose where they grew. At least here she would be a feature. 'We'll meet by the tree,' people would say.

Maybe, when Floss did come back, she would meet someone by the tree. And maybe she wouldn't want to leave it. Maybe, without knowing why, she'd want to stay at the airport, want to sit beside the tree she didn't realise she knew. Maybe she'd remember Cassie when she saw the tree. Maybe she would remember loving her. When she came back.

Jake.

THE GIRL, DELIA, WAS EATING with one hand and using the other to flip through Jake's photos. Jake had never seen an adult eat like that, not at dinner time. She hadn't said anything in a while, but she kept glancing at the empty chair. Jake had the impression she was trying hard not to say anything.

'Why are you looking at those pictures instead of talking to me?' the empty chair said suddenly.

Delia smiled to herself and looked up. 'Oh, you should look at them too.'

Jake's mouth felt dry suddenly as Delia pushed the pile of photos across the table.

'Are these yours?' the empty chair asked.

'No,' said Delia. 'They're someone else's. They're good, aren't they?'

'I like this one of the dog. I think this dog lives around here.'

Jake had hated the dog next door for months. He hated most dogs these days; they reminded him of bad things. Then he'd decided to take photos of it and had spent an entire hot Sunday perched on top of the back garden wall leaning over as far as he dared with his camera. By the end of the day, he and the dog understood each other.

Jake sat listening to his dad talk as he went through his photos. He noticed that the girl Delia had stopped eating and was gripping the table. She kept looking at Jake, and he kept nodding at her to let her know that he could hear what his dad was saying.

'Hey,' said the chair, 'I've seen these ones before. These ones at the zoo.'

'I took those ages ago,' said Jake. 'Months and months ago.'

'What was that?' said the empty chair, which for a moment was not empty.

Delia, sat up straight and looked at Jake. Jake chewed his lip and sank down in his seat. He was suddenly afraid, but he didn't know why. He hadn't been afraid in the longest of times. Not since those moments on that day. The ones before he knew he had nothing left to lose.

'What?' said Delia.

'Someone said something. It wasn't you, it was someone else.'

'It was Jake,' said Delia. Jake swallowed twice.

'What?'

'Jake, Anthony. Your son. He took those photos months ago.'

Anthony stood up from the table. 'Do you want dessert?' he said. 'I think I have ice cream.'

'Oh, for fuck's sake,' said Delia. 'Sure, fine, but don't you want to keep looking at the photos?'

'Oh, that's OK; they might get dirty. We shouldn't really have them at the table. You'll have to give them back to the person who took them, right?'

'Your fucking son took them, idiot! Sorry Jake.'

Jake didn't say anything. He got up from the table and walked around to where his dad had been sitting. He slipped the pile of photos off the table and carried them out of the room. He heard Delia calling after him, but he kept walking, up the stairs and into his room. He put the photos back into the shoebox he kept them in and sat on his bed, looking at his collection.

It had been days since he'd found a lost thing. That was probably why he felt so sad.

The Wedding Certificate.

ITEM: MARRIAGE CERTIFICATE

Place found: living room cupboard.

The month on the certificate was April. The place was Akaroa, New Zealand. The names were Holly Grey and Anthony Baxter.

It had been packed in a large box with a lot of other papers, where it had stayed for several months. When the box was unpacked and the bank statements and bills and letters filed in sensible places, the certificate was left out for a while. Its owner didn't know what he was supposed to do with it.

Eventually, he slipped it into the cupboard, resolving to find a more appropriate place. But other things were added to the cupboard and the certificate got lost beneath them.

Every once in a while, the owner would remember it, and resolve to search for it, to find it, and decide how it should be kept.

Mrs Featherby.

THE SHEET OF PLASTIC WAS down. If Mrs Featherby had been overseeing its removal, it would have been folded immediately, pressed and put in its rightful place in whatever closet was designated for the storing of house-sized plastic sheeting. But it was Bruno who was in charge, and so the sheet was draped over the small front garden, forming dirty white mountains and valleys, spilling out over the low stone wall and onto the footpath and road beyond.

The sheet of plastic was down because a wall was going up. Mrs Featherby stood in her sitting room, watching as bricks were laid and mortar was spread. When the wall was up to her waist, a small girl appeared on the other side of it.

'Good afternoon, Small Girl Bonny,' she said.

'Hello,' returned the girl, with serious eyes. 'Is your house being fixed?'

'It certainly is.'

'Oh. Will I still be able to get into it?'

'I dare say you will. There is going to be a door.'

The two of them stood, facing each other, as the wall rose. As it covered Small Girl Bonny's face, she called over it, 'Goodbye, um, Mrs.'

Mrs Featherby remained silent as the wall continued to rise. After a few minutes Small Girl Bonny's voice sailed over again.

'Oh, that's right, my mum says you can come over to my house for dinner now because of all the building. Not right now. At dinner time.'

Mrs Featherby swallowed and took a moment before she spoke. Before she could trust herself to speak.

'Thank you, Small Girl Bonny. That sounds delightful and I'll certainly try to make it.'

Jake.

THE LOST LETTER WASN'T REALLY lost. It had just gone wrong. It had been in the normal pile of mail that came every morning, but it was in the pile at Jake's house instead of the pile it was supposed to be in at someone else's house.

The address was hard to read and the postcode was missing.

The letter sat on the floor of his room for weeks, in between a one-armed stuffed gorilla and a set of car keys, and Jake wanted to open it. He could see where the letter had come from and it was a long way away. He could see how it had become jumbled up with all the other letters and gone into the wrong pile. He could see how it had made its way to his house instead of the other house, the right house. But he wanted to see which house it was. He wanted to see who was supposed to get the letter instead of him, and he thought that maybe if he opened it, and if he looked inside it, then he'd know.

He wanted to be useful. He wanted to matter. He never used to think about whether or not he mattered. But now he had vanished to the person who mattered most to him. If his father couldn't see him, he wouldn't worry about him being gone, and Jake could be useful to someone else.

It was wrong to open other people's mail. Jake knew that it was wrong. But if he didn't open it, he thought, it would never get to the right person. And wasn't that worse?

Just like he'd done dozens of times before, he picked up the letter from its position on the floor, amongst the clutter of loss. The flap was peeling off at the edges from the picking of Jake's fingers.

Someone was waiting for this letter, he knew. Someone was desperate for it. Someone was lost without it.

Jake sat on his bed, his thumb flicking against the flap, wondering what to do. If only it would come loose completely. If it opened on its own it would be OK. If it opened on its own it wasn't his fault.

But it didn't open.

Jake stared at the envelope. He pushed his finger into the gap in the corner and pulled a little. A tear appeared, snaking tantalisingly down the front of the envelope. Jake could see the thin, folded paper inside.

With a grimace, he widened the tear and pulled the letter out. Holding it in his hand, he tried to see where it had been going. He could see pictures – vague images that disappeared almost immediately – but he couldn't see anything definite. He couldn't see anything helpful.

There was something Jake's mum used to say that Jake had never really understood. She used to say it just after she'd eaten a chocolate biscuit and really wanted to have another one. She would say 'hung for a penny'. Jake had never asked his mum what it meant, apart from that you got to eat a second chocolate biscuit, but he remembered it as he looked at the folded piece of paper in his hand.

After you've opened a letter, no one will believe you didn't read it.

'Hung for a penny,' he whispered to himself as he unfolded the letter.

He looked at the letter for a moment, without taking in much of what was on it. He knew where to go. He knew who the letter was for. He'd seen her. He'd talked to her. He knew where to go.

Cassie.

THERE IS A TREE IN Terminal Two of Heathrow Airport. Were it in a glen, or on a hill, or by a river, as it should be, it would provide shelter from the sun and rain. Under it, children could play, lovers could kiss, the weary could rest. But it is not in a glen, or on a hill, or by a river, it is in an airport, under harsh artificial light, partially obscuring the arrivals board.

There is grass spreading out from the tree; it almost reaches the far corners of the room, and in some places there are flowers. Benches and chairs and tables that used to be moveable have grown into the floor.

There are complaints and mutterings about the difficulty of reading the arrivals announcements, about the challenge of pulling a suitcase along in a grassy area, but really people tend to smile at the sight of a tree in such an unusual place.

It is a reminder that the world is not quite as we expect it to be.

There is little wind in Terminal Two of Heathrow Airport, but sometimes a breeze seems to ripple through the tree's leaves.

There are no birds in Terminal Two of Heathrow Airport, but some kind of life seems to live there, although the few who are aware of this enough to consider it, cannot fathom what that life is.

There is a tree in Terminal Two of Heathrow Airport, where no tree should be.

Robert.

Robert stood in the kitchen not helping Mara make cannelloni for dinner.

He stood in the kitchen not drinking the cup of tea that was sitting on the bench.

He stood in the kitchen not answering the questions his daughter was asking him about trains.

He hadn't realised visiting Mara's father had been restful. He hadn't noticed that his mood had changed. He hadn't noticed it changing on the flight out of London and he hadn't noticed it changing over the days they spent on the beach, but he had noticed it as the flight home began its descent.

It was as if the plane was flying into a field of nothingness that weighed a tonne. As though there was a toxic cloud over the city, which seeped into the plane through the walls and into Robert through his skin.

He hadn't noticed how little he'd been talking since he and his girls had got home. He hadn't noticed how often Mara was looking at him or how many questions Bonny was asking.

He didn't notice Mara saying his name six times as she chopped tomatoes. He didn't notice her wave her arms at him across the kitchen.

He did notice when she put the point of her knife against his throat.

'What?' he said. 'What is it?'

'If you're not helping me here, and believe me you're not,' said Mara, 'would you mind going over the street and getting Mrs Featherby?'

Robert stood in the middle of the road outside his house. The street looked somehow unfamiliar.

The last time he'd stood this long in the middle of this street was the day Bonny was born. He and Mara had been moving into the house. They were all excitement and expectation until they had been waiting four hours for the delivery van to show up. They'd stood in the middle of the road, both too cross to even hold hands, looking in opposite directions, each hoping they'd be the first to spot it.

Robert had seen the van rounding his corner and been just about to crow at Mara, when she'd grabbed his hand more tightly than she'd ever grabbed it before.

'My waters have broken,' she whispered, almost too quietly to hear.

'The van's here,' Robert had replied.

'What?' Mara had said.

'What, wait, *what*?'

'My bloody *waters* have mother fucking *broken*, and you're rabbiting on about some shit-encrusted *van*, what *van*, why do we care about a *van*, I'm about to push a *whole entire living human* out of my *cunting cunt,* and you don't even seem to care, and holy shit this wasn't a good idea. Why are we doing this? This is a stupid thing to do. I've changed my mind.'

Robert paused for a moment and swallowed.

'Right,' he said, 'Of course. It's fine. I was just distracted because the moving van's here, but that's fine. Let's just get you to the hospital.'

'The moving van?'

'The moving van. With everything we own inside it.'

'Oh. Shit.'

And then:

'Oooooh shiiiiit.'

'I know.'

'Oh my *god.*'

'I know.'

'No, fuck you, shut up, you don't know, I just had my first *contraction.*'

'Oh. Oh shit.'

The van had pulled up at the kerb by this point, and the driver was stepping out.

'Man, sorry about the wait, complete mare of an accident on Waterloo Bridge.'

'Fuck *off.*'

'Why the fuck did you come via – no, sorry, Mara's just gone into labour, um, we're going to have to leave now.'

'Oh,' said the driver, whose name was Sam, and whose experience of childbirth was limited. 'Oh fuck.'

'*No,*' said Mara, shooting the driver with hypothetical eye lasers. 'You do not get to swear. All the swearing is *mine.*'

'Look,' said Robert, 'here's a set of keys. Pile it all in there as best you can and chuck them through the letter box, all right? Great, thanks, good luck.'

The van driver was still staring after them as Robert drove round the corner ill-advisedly fast.

'Fuck,' said Mara, in the seat beside him. 'Fuckfuck*fuck*fuckfuck. Holy mother fucking shit.'

'Wow. Is it hurting?'

'No, not at the moment, I'm just freaking right out. I can't do this.'

'Of course you can.'

'How do you know that?'

'Well –' Robert had paused, '– it's the only option, really.'

Robert stared at the ground, pretending he could see a stain from Mara's waters breaking. He couldn't, of course; he hadn't even been able to see it when he came home that night, but he liked to think it was there still, invisibly. Bonny's birth part of the street for ever.

He gave a start, suddenly remembering what he was meant to be doing, and continued across the road. It took him a moment to remember which house he was aiming for; it looked a lot less distinctive now that it was missing a lot less wall. He approached the new front door and knocked.

He wasn't sure how long he'd been waiting when it occurred to him to knock again.

After a couple of tries he peered through the nearest new window. It looked like the furniture was covered in sheets and the room was dim.

Robert went back to the front door and chewed his lip. After a moment he noticed a small note stuck on the door at hip height. He pulled it off.

'Small Girl Bonny,' it read. 'I will see you again.'

Robert stood there in the dark, outside the empty house.

Jake.

JAKE WASN'T SUPPOSED TO GET the tube on his own. When he had first arrived in London and he hadn't started school yet, he'd had to ride the tube to get to some places. He'd gone to the Tower of London, where he'd heard stories about the two little princes who disappeared, and about all the different imprisoned queens. He'd gone to the park, the giant park, and he'd seen deer. He'd gone to Buckingham Palace, which didn't look anything like what a palace was supposed to look like.

But he hadn't gone alone.

Someone had gone with him.

Then, he'd wanted to find things. And he couldn't see the someone who was supposed to take him.

Jake thought back to his first rides on the tube. Don't run for the train, he'd been told, and don't lean on the doors. Stand on the right-hand side when you're on the escalator. Make sure you go to the right platform.

His dad had told him that.

Jake could picture his dad telling him how to ride the tube more clearly than he could see him in real life.

He went through the barrier and waited at the lift. He was the only person in the station. He looked carefully at the list of stations the train went to and headed to the platform.

The journey was long and he had to change trains but he got there.

The airport was busy and loud and full of people. Some of them looked at Jake, some of them seemed puzzled and worried, but he kept walking. He had somewhere to be. He walked towards Terminal Two, to the arrivals gate.

He went to where he was supposed to go, to where the letter was needed, but there was no one there. There was no person there.

The floor of the airport was covered in grass, and in the place where Jake was taking the letter there was only a tree.

He wasn't prepared for this. You can't give a letter to a tree, after all.

He sat on the floor by the tree, where it would have been spreading shade if it had been out in the open where it belonged, instead of shut up inside an airport. Jake sat on the floor with the letter in his hand and he thought about what he should do.

Marcus.

HE HAD A STRANGER'S HANDS. For weeks now he'd had a stranger's hands. Their joints wouldn't bend the way he wanted them
to — they would send sharp pains through him, as though in
punishment. They didn't look like his hands either, the fingers
seemed shorter, squatter, less communicative than they should be.

Even his handwriting was different. He used to write in a long,
slender dance of elegant illegibility. Now, out of nowhere, round
but cramped letters had started appearing, muddling the sense of
his words.

There was a letter he wanted to write. It was the only thing he
could think to do with himself.

> *Dear Brown-Haired Woman,*
>   *I apologise, I have forgotten your name.*
>   *Yes. Yes, I will give lessons to your daughter.*
>   *I will not charge. I have no need of money.*
>   *I will call at your home on Wednesday at 4pm.*
> *Yours,*
> *Marcus Weber*

He delivered the letter by hand, early in the morning before anyone
was around.

This, he thought, couldn't be something to hang on to.

Afterwards he sat in his music room, by the window, trying to write another letter. A letter to his best loved. But it felt like it wasn't him in the letter at all.

Most Wondrous of Katharines,

It is hard for me to use words, but easier this way than speaking. And what I have to say is important, for it is from not only me, but from your other father. Your better father.

You were my gift to him, you see. He wanted you so much, and I wasn't sure. We were too old, I thought, and had I known that I would be the one you were left with last, I would have fought that battle harder, I think. I am glad I didn't know. For many reasons, of course, but for you most of all.

I could never have made Albert as happy alone as you were able to make him. I could never have recovered after his death, if you were not there to recover for.

It is not just that you have been the greatest joy to me, and to your other father before he was lost, rather you have been the thing that has brought the greatest joy to every part of our lives.

You are wonderful. You are glorious.
Your loving father, Marcus.

He sealed the letter in an envelope. He didn't know that this was his last opportunity to write it, but he didn't know that it wasn't either. He walked into the room he now so rarely entered. He crossed to his fractured piano and raised the lip. Trying not to hit one of the keys – the keys that were not his, the keys that were not right – he set the letter down and closed the lid over it. She would find it later.

He could no longer rely on himself. He was no longer enough. He couldn't sustain himself. He knew it was coming.

He had now only to wait.

Robert.

THE DAY WAS CLEAR AND lovely and Mara had decided to stop working at twelve. She'd ordered Robert to pack a picnic, so he spent the better part of the morning on salads, breads and an apple pie.

They sat on a rug, took turns chasing Bonny in dizzying circles, and ate slowly and luxuriously, with no regard for the passage of time.

'I've decided something,' Mara said suddenly, when Bonny had become distracted by the passage of a ladybird over the corner of their rug.

'You want to give up your career and join a burlesque troop?' said Robert.

'Well, obviously, but I think I can save that for retirement.'

'You've all of a sudden developed a passion for shellfish?'

Mara gave a grimace that passed over her entire body.

'All right,' said Robert. 'I've no idea. In my mind they were the only two possibilities. What's up?'

'I don't want us to live in London anymore.'

Robert was silent for a moment, watching his daughter try to coax the ladybird off the rug and onto her finger. He wanted to warn the bug away; the finger of a five-year-old girl is a safe place for no one.

'You don't want us to live in London?' he said. 'Not you don't want to live in London yourself, but you don't want us as a family to live here?'

'Yeah,' Mara said. She was looking at Robert, but not in his eyes. 'I think it would be a good time for us to be somewhere else. For a while. Just a year, maybe, or two.'

'Have I done this?'

'Well, kind of, but that's not a bad thing. Moving isn't a bad thing. We could go anywhere. We could live by the sea for a while. We could even try living in a different country. I can work anywhere, obviously, and you're, you know . . . transitioning. We could go somewhere exciting, with cliffs and wind, or somewhere pleasant, with meadows. We could get both somewhere, probably. You can finish carving all the woodwork into hideousness in our house, and then we'll bugger off.'

Robert sat up and began packing away the plates.

'Let's not go yet,' said Mara. 'It's a nice day.'

'I'm worried it's going to start getting too cold for Bonny. We didn't bring her a warm jersey, that cardigan's all she's got.'

'She's fine. Are you cold, Bonny?'

'No,' said their girl. 'Did we bring a kite?'

'No,' said Mara. 'We should have. What happened to the kite?'

'It's broken, remember?' said Robert. 'Last time we flew it, it crashed.'

'Right. Well, we should get a new one.' Mara took out the Thermos Robert had just packed in the basket and poured herself another coffee. 'We never wanted to live here for ever, did we? We never wanted to stay. Besides, we have to get out of that hideous house, with all its crazy vine carvings.'

'I just didn't want leaving to be my fault.'

'It's not your fault.'

'Well it's not yours. It's not Bonny's. I lost my job, which is bad enough, and then I got all obsessive and needy about it, which makes the whole thing worse. I've made the house all strange and toxic with my worry, the house where you have to work and Bonny has to learn. You've decided that the only way to get me over myself is to move all of us to god knows where so I can't spend all my energy not going into work. Right?'

Mara sat cross-legged, languorously sipping her coffee, leaning back on one arm. 'I'm not trying to fix you, Rob. I'm not saying you need fixing. I think this isn't a good place for us to be, just at the moment. So we should go.'

'"For us". Not for you, not for Bonny. Just for me, which means it has to be not a good place for all of us.'

'That's the deal, sweet pea. That's how it works.'

Robert groaned and passed a hand over his face. The idea of leaving, of leaving everything so unresolved, of giving up on the idea of his job ever reappearing, of vanishing into the distance terrified him. A pair of tiny arms encircled his neck.

'Dad, I need a piggyback ride just now,' Bonny said in his ear.

'You kids go nuts,' said Mara. 'I brought a book.'

Robert felt a surge of frustration. It didn't seem OK to still have not figured out what to do. It didn't seem right or fair. Mara seemed so calm and sure.

He had never felt so uncertain. There was so little in his life he was sure of.

'Dad,' said Bonny, tightening her grip on him. 'Come on. Play with me.'

Robert lifted his daughter high into the air.

Delia.

THERE WAS NO ONE AT the house when Delia got there. It was
the first time Jake hadn't been at home. The first evening he'd not
been waiting for her to arrive. She knocked on the door every five
minutes for almost an hour, growing more and more frantic.

Finally, she turned away from her latest attempt to get inside
to see Anthony coming up the path. At the sight of him she burst
into tears.

'Hey,' he said, moving quickly towards her and putting his
hands on either side of her face. 'What's wrong?'

Delia grabbed the front of his shirt and pulled herself up onto her
toes, her eyes fixed on his. 'Where is he?' she said. 'Where is Jake?'

'What is it, Delia? Why are you so upset?'

Delia shook him a little bit. 'Anthony. You have a son. Where
is your son?'

'Come on, you know you can talk to me.'

Delia took a breath and let go. 'Just let me in. Let me into the
house.'

Once Anthony had opened the door she pushed past him and
started charging through the house. There were photos everywhere,
slotted in the sides of every picture frame, pinned to walls, doors,
and windows, resting on shelves, spread over tables. There were
also notes and drawings. As he caught sight of them, Anthony
squinted his eyes and shook his head a little. He walked over to
the fridge. There was a large, poster-like note that said 'Hiya Dad'

in large green letters. He pulled it off and held it, gazing down at it, his brow furrowed.

'Anthony,' said Delia. He took a moment to look up and when he did, for a moment it was as if she were the one he couldn't see.

He swallowed twice.

'Anthony,' said Delia again. 'Where is he?'

It took him a moment to speak. 'I don't know.'

Delia spun on her heel and headed into the hall. She climbed the stairs and raced into Jake's room. Anthony was only a few steps behind.

The room was small and incredibly messy, although not with the normal clutter of a prepubescent boy. Scattered over the floor, falling off shelves, spilling out of drawers was a collection of miscellany; a battered leather notebook, a single pearl earring, an ostentatious perfume bottle.

'What is all this?' said Anthony.

'Jake's collection,' said Delia. 'He likes collecting lost things.'

'Where does he find it all?'

'I don't know. Around. I suppose.'

'What—'

'It doesn't matter right now, Anthony. What matters is, where is he? When was the last time you saw him?'

Anthony was silent for a moment. 'Oh my god.'

'Yes,' said Delia. 'Yes, exactly.'

She turned and headed for the door.

'Where are you going?' Anthony called after her.

'To find your son, obviously.'

'You don't know where to look. And even if you did know, you wouldn't know how to get there.'

'That doesn't matter. This is more important than my ludicrous inability to find my way anywhere at all.'

'You're not making any sense,' Anthony called down the stairs after her, but Delia was already halfway out the door. He caught up to her as she approached the corner of the street.

'Where are you going?'

'I told you.'

'Delia, this isn't the way to look for him. We should go back to the house and try to figure out where he'd be likely to go.'

'You can do that if you want. I'm going to walk to the end of this street. And when I get there, I'm going to turn right.'

'Why?'

'Because it's the right way to go.'

'To get where?'

'Don't know.'

'I don't—'

Delia stopped walking and looked at Anthony. He was pale, and suddenly seemed a lot older than he normally did. His eyes were red and he kept swallowing. This was a man who couldn't find his son and whose girlfriend was suddenly acting crazy.

'Anthony,' she said. 'Please just trust me.'

'But what if you're wrong?'

'What if we assume that and we go back and spend hours and hours trying to figure out where Jake could have gone, which, given that I've only met the boy a few times and you've become physically unable to see him, promises to be a difficult task, but what if we do it anyway, what if we spend hours listing vague possibilities, and what if we check them all and he's not there and we end up criss-crossing vaguely all over London for ever and ever, and we could have just found him today because I know where to go, and also why in god's name does the boy not have a mobile?'

'I – he's too young. He's not allowed one till he's older. Till he's old enough to go out on his own.'

'I'm going this way. You're welcome to join me.'

Anthony stood there, looking so worried, looking so suddenly tired.

'I just don't believe you really know the way,' he said.

'I don't care what you believe, I'm going this way. You don't have to come. But if you do, if it'll make you happier, we can try to think of places he might have gone while we walk.'

Anthony still looked upset and doubt-ridden, but he nodded once and walked on. His sudden agreement gave Delia a moment of disquiet. What if she was wrong? How could she possibly know which way to go?

It was like driving along a winding road in thick fog. She only knew what to do next, not what to do after that, and she had no idea of the end destination. What if suddenly she didn't know the next step? What if she was sure the whole way until they arrived somewhere and found she was wrong?

She led Anthony through the winding streets of the neighbourhood until they arrived at a bus stop. Anthony gave her a querying look and went to get on the bus that had just pulled up. Delia shook her head. They waited.

After ten minutes another bus arrived and this one was right. Delia didn't know when they'd have to get off the bus, or how quickly she'd know to, so they stood near the door.

'Here,' Delia said as the bus pulled up outside the tube station, and headed down to the platform, Anthony following. They changed at Kings Cross and sat in silence as the train moved on.

'Do you know yet,' Anthony asked after a while. 'Do you know where he is? Actually?'

'No,' said Delia. 'Are we getting close to somewhere you think he'd go?'

'He doesn't know this side of London at all.'

They were silent again as they went through a few more stations, getting further and further west.

'Oh my god,' said Anthony suddenly. 'We're practically at Heathrow.'

'Why would he go to the airport?'

'To go home.'

'No. He can't have thought he'd be able to go home. He's old enough to know you can't just fly away to the antipodes on a moment's notice. And he hasn't taken your credit card has he?'

'I lost my credit card three weeks ago.'

'Oh my god.'

'I just assumed I'd left it somewhere around the house, I do that all the time. I've been meaning to have a proper look for it, but I just – it didn't seem important.'

'You are a disaster. It's been disguised all this time by how much of a disaster I am, but actually you, you're worse.'

'How have I done this?' said Anthony. 'How have I let this happen?'

'You just didn't put your card back in your wallet like a sensible grown up.'

'No. How did I let him disappear? There must have been a point when I saw what was happening. I must have noticed he was fading. I must have noticed and done nothing.'

Delia was silent.

'I know it's my fault.'

'That's not going to help anyone, though, is it?'

'What if we find him, what if we find him right now, and I still can't see him?'

For a moment Delia wanted nothing more than to run away. This was too hard, it was too much. She wasn't equipped for dealing with real human emotions, with real fear and brokenness. She had a long history of ignoring feelings until they went away.

'I don't know,' she said. 'I don't know.'

Delia and Anthony sat still and silent in the crowded tube carriage. It pulled into the station for Heathrow. Anthony looked at Delia, his eyebrows raised in enquiry. She nodded and they stepped out and headed for the escalator.

Anthony was still looking pale and frightened.

'Maybe I'm wrong,' said Delia. 'You think I'm wrong, remember?'

He didn't answer. He rode the escalator to the top and waited for Delia to lead the way.

'Hey,' he said after a while, 'you're going the wrong way.'

'No, I'm not.'

'But you're heading to arrivals.'

'I'm heading to Jake.'

'What? What do you mean?'

'I don't know, Anthony, I just know it's true.'

Delia gasped as she turned the corner into the arrivals area. She was suddenly standing on sparse but vibrant grass; the terminal looked like a wild garden. And over in the distance, growing where the grass was thickest, was a small tree.

Delia could see someone underneath it, curled up and still.

Jake.

Jake stands on the footpath facing his house. He waits for his
    mum to come back out to take him to the doctor.
He doesn't know. If he knew, he would have gone in with her.
If he knew, he wouldn't have let her go in at all. If he knew, he
would run inside now and find her. He would drag her outside.
He would hold everything up so she could get out. He would
    just hug her.
He doesn't know. He doesn't know he's seen her for the last time.
    He's excited about having the day off school. It feels like he's
breaking the rules, even though it's his mother that's making him.
    He doesn't want to go to the doctor, he never wants to go to
the doctor, he hates his stupid foot for making him, but he's
glad to not be at school. He's excited about getting a sundae at
    McDonald's.
His mum's taking a long time to come out of the house and
he's getting bored. He doesn't care if she finds the recipe she
needs or not, he just doesn't like waiting. He doesn't even know
    why his mum is so worried about remembering to bring a
recipe for a lady she doesn't even like. He thinks that when he's
grown up and no one is telling him what to do anymore he
    won't be nice to anyone except his friends.
He looks up at the sky. It is grey and uninteresting. When he
was a much littler kid, last year, the weather had done interesting things. There had been thunderstorms and snow and days

so hot your ice cream melted before you had a chance to eat it. Now the weather never did anything fun. Who even cares about the weather anyway?

Jake scowls and glares at the front door. He doesn't care about getting to the doctor, but the faster they do that, the sooner there'll be ice cream.

The first thing he notices is the roof. It ripples and surges as if it's made of water. The road and the footpath he stands on do the same thing. He grabs the lamppost and he doesn't fall down. The roof isn't made to ripple like that. The walls can't hold it together. Jake can do nothing, he can't even speak, he can't call out. The house falls, the house his mother has gone back into, the house she hasn't yet come back from, falls.

And Jake is left alone.

Jake had fallen asleep and woken up and fallen asleep and woken up more times than he knew as he sat under the tree at Heathrow Airport. He didn't know why he was staying there; he didn't know what he was waiting for. The person who needed the letter was gone now, she was changed, and there was no reason to think she'd change back. But he didn't want to take it away again. It was too important.

Jake doesn't bother to open his eyes; there's nothing new to see. He sits still and folds and unfolds the letter.

Cassie,
   I'm coming. Soon.
Floss.

He has no idea how long he's been waiting.

His back is resting against the tree, and so he knows the tree is lost. He knows that it arrived at the airport and got lost there, and he knows that people still are afraid of it. They leave it alone, although they didn't always.

Jake doesn't hear anyone approach him. The grass is thick where he is and hides the sound, so he doesn't realise anyone's there at first.

'Jake,' someone says. Someone familiar. Someone important.

'Jake, are you all right?'

Jake opens his eyes.

'Hi Dad,' he says. 'Hi.'

'Are you OK?'

'I'm OK. I was just thinking.'

'What are you doing here?'

'I had to bring something. I was supposed to give it to someone but there's no one here.'

There was someone with his dad, standing just behind him. The girl. Delia.

'Can you come home please, Jake?' said his dad. 'We've been really worried about you.'

'Can I wait a bit longer? In case they come?'

Jake's dad looked worried for a moment. 'I suppose,' he said eventually. 'If I can wait with you. Will you tell me about it all?'

Delia.

DELIA STOOD A COUPLE OF feet away from the bizarre tree that was standing at the arrivals gate of Terminal Two of Heathrow Airport. She was watching Jake and Anthony talk as they sat side by side, half concealed by branches. They looked so alike, and so engrossed.

She turned to go.

'Delia,' Anthony called. 'Where are you going?'

She smiled, a little, almost. She almost smiled. 'Home,' she said. 'This story's just for you.'

'You won't find your way.'

'I actually think I will,' said Delia. 'I have a good feeling.'

She smiled properly this time, once at Anthony and once at Jake, and walked away.

Under the tree, Anthony stared after her. He glanced down at his son. 'What a woman,' he said.

And the branches around them rustled.

Acknowledgements.

WHEN I WAS WRITING AND re-writing this book, I was too broke to have had any fun were it not for the excellent people who were willing to pay for my drinks and food and tickets to things. So, thanks to Jamie, Adam, Mike, Brendan, Jonno, Serena, Annie, Jav, Matt, Fran, Kat, Caroline, Lucy, Duncan, Joel, Sacha, Jon, others I've probably forgotten, and more than anyone else, my mum, for the fun times I couldn't afford on my own.

Also thanks to Amy Grace, Erin Simpson and the collected Matthewsons for jumping on my bandwagon when there was no promise of it leading anywhere, and to Jamie Drew for absorbing all my unfiltered emotions.

Finally, giddy and incredulous thanks to Scott, Rachel and Cicely at the Friday Project, and all the delightful people at HarperCollins.

About the author.

JANINA MATTHEWSON GREW UP IN New Zealand, where she studied theatre and linguistics. She has been living in London for three years, along with half the population of New Zealand. She is the author of *The Understanding of Women*, which is a fictional novella, not an instructional guide. As well as prose, she has also written a one-act play, *Human and If*, and several short films.